VOODOO YOU THINK YOU ARE

A MALVEAUX CURSE MYSTERY (BOOK 5)

G.A. CHASE

BAYOU MOON PRESS, LLC

Copyright © 2017 by G.A. Chase

First Edition 2017

Cover Art by Janet Holmes

Editing by Red Adept

ISBN eBook: 978-1-940299-49-5

ISBN Print: 978-1-940299-48-8

Bayou Moon Press, LLC

ABOUT THIS BOOK

Kendell Summer is finally settled into her new French Quarter apartment with her boyfriend, Myles, and their two pups, Cheesecake and Doughnut Hole. Life would be perfect if it weren't for the swamp witch Sanguine, who is still lying comatose—after losing her soul—on their new couch like Sleeping Beauty.

With no idea how to help her sleeping friend, Kendell carries on with her nightly gigs as lead guitarist for Polly Urethane and the Strippers. But when each one of her bandmates slumps to the stage floor, exhausted, due to a lingering connection to Sanguine's missing soul, Myles realizes the swamp witch is sapping them dry.

With the band in danger, it's a race against the clock while Kendell and Myles work to find and restore the swamp witch's spirit. To Kendell's consternation, however, Sanguine doesn't want to be rescued. As hell's angel,

Sanguine is busy dealing with the devil they've all had a hand in creating.

One thing is clear: someone had better do something soon because Colin has amassed enough power to blast his way out of hell and rejoin the land of the living.

Kendell Summer set her jet-black electric guitar back in its onstage stand. The simple act transformed her from her onstage persona of Olympia Stain, lead guitarist for Polly Urethane and the Strippers, back to the person she normally was.

"My fingers hurt like I haven't played in a month." It had been two weeks since she, the band, and her boyfriend, Myles, had returned from hell, but playing before a live crowd still made her attack her guitar with so much vigor she shredded the strings.

She turned away from the crowd, wondering why none of her bandmates had responded to her whining. The lingering humidity of early fall, combined with the smell of endorphins and sweat from the crowd, would dim anyone's lights, but from the way the women huddled on the stage speakers, Kendell feared their silence wasn't due simply to exhaustion.

"What's wrong with you guys?"

Their drummer, Minerva Wax, lifted her hand. Her quivering fingers didn't look capable of grasping a drumstick, let alone hammering out the blues-punk standards. "I feel like I'm having a fucking heart attack."

Scraper, their bass player, didn't look much better. "We played hard, no doubt, but I'm with Minerva. There's something wrong with me."

Lynn Seed was usually the spunky pick-me-up when everyone else was down, but she only stared at her shaking fingers. "I barely made it through that last number. I was certain the keyboard was shifting around like an earthquake was happening."

"This is stupid." In defiance of the band's exhaustion, Polly tried to stand up. She slumped to the ground at Lynn's feet.

Kendell jumped offstage and ran to the bar, where Myles was opening a couple of beers for some inebriated customers. "Can Charlie take over for a minute? I need you." She hoped her tone wouldn't alarm any of the club's patrons.

From the look on Myles's face, she could tell that he got her subtle message of concern. "Of course."

As he came out from behind the bar, she took his hand and rushed him to the stage. "I'd say it was food poisoning, but we all ate from the same Lucky Dog cart."

He didn't bother asking how they felt. "Let's get you women out back for a little fresh air."

Anyone listening in would assume that was all they

needed. Lynn and Polly leaned on his shoulders as he guided them out the back door to the courtyard. Minerva and Scraper fared slightly better, relying on each other for support.

Kendell hopped back onstage and grabbed the microphone. "We're going to take a little break. Hang around for the Mutants at Table Nine, who'll take the stage shortly."

By the time she joined up with the band, Myles had already fetched some rum from his hidden speakeasy to help calm the women.

"What do you think is happening?" Kendell asked.

He motioned her toward a metal chair. "Their problem isn't physical. I can feel it too, but the energy flow isn't draining me. I'm just the conduit."

The cool night breeze that chilled Kendell's sweat-covered skin was like a ghost tapping her on the shoulder. "You don't mean Sanguine?" Though Sanguine's body lie in repose on their couch, her spirit had yet to be found.

Myles had only been psychically connected to the band members once while in hell. Funneling their combined spiritual energy into Sanguine had given the young swamp witch the power to lure Colin's demonic animals away from Kendell.

Polly set her empty glass on the table. "We were only bonded to her for a short time—not long enough for me to feel drained. But now that you mention it, I've been a little out of sorts since we got home."

The other women nodded. The trip to hell to confront

Colin Malveaux in his realm without time had affected everyone's sleep habits. Even Cheesecake and her puppy Doughnut Hole had only been able to get three hours of continuous sleep. Each night, they got up and stalked the apartment like sentries convinced of an intruder.

"Are you sure it's not just fatigue?" Kendell asked.

Myles pulled his chair closer to the table. "There's one way to find out. If I connect to you all the way I did in hell, I might be able to detect what's happening in your souls."

Though she trusted him with more than just her life, Kendell hated the idea of him connecting his soul to anyone but her. "But you can't contact Sanguine. We already tried. If she's trapped in hell with Colin, she'll be isolated from all other human spirits."

Lynn twirled her glass on the table like a little child about to annoy her mother. "We could take a peek."

If they hadn't brought Sanguine's comatose body out of hell, Kendell would have been perfectly happy to ignore the seven gates they'd created connecting hell to life. The likelihood that her friend was trapped in the hell created by Sanguine's grandmother, however, had Kendell wondering if she'd ever be free of the Malveaux curse that had started her voodoo journey.

"You guys guard the second gate in there onstage, Myles the fifth gate back here at the speakeasy, and I watch over the seventh gate at Scratch and Sniff," Kendell said. "Unless Colin or Sanguine happen to be passing by one of those locations, I'm not sure what good it would do to open ourselves to hell's nightmares."

Scraper reached for the bottle of rum and refilled her

glass. "We have to do something. I barely made it through the gig tonight. If Sanguine is sapping our souls, someone's going to have to tell her to knock it off. If it's not her, then we all need some kind of voodoo NyQuil."

It was a testament to how tired the band was that Scraper's comment didn't set off a round of bad jokes.

Myles refilled his glass with slow deliberation. His precise movements were a sure indication he was about to say something Kendell wasn't going to like. "You shouldn't use the seventh gate as a window into hell. You're too connected to Colin. Even with your power over the curse isolated in the golden pick we left in hell, I worry that he'll detect you somehow. I'm still freaked out about how he was able to access our ceremony that formed the gates."

Though Kendell didn't like being told what to do or what not to do, he had a point. Seeing Colin's smug face while the guardians of the seven gates united their souls to watch over him left her with the uneasy suspicion that hell wasn't as secure as it should be. And without Sanguine, Kendell was solely in charge.

"So you check on your gate and the band checks on theirs while I twiddle my thumbs?" she asked.

"It's a start, and relative to my other ideas, it's the least likely to suck us all into another interdimensional escapade."

She hated admitting he was right, but she hated even more the idea of him taking on a risk without her. "Take Doughnut Hole with you. Polly can bring Muffin Top, and Lynn can bring Cupcake. At least with hell's puppies, I'll feel like you're being protected."

Scraper held her head like a drunk feeling the alcohol wear off. "I can't handle digging into Colin's activities tonight. I need a few hours of sleep, though I doubt it'll help. I suggest we reconvene first thing in the morning."

～

MYLES WALKED with Kendell back to their apartment while enjoying the serenade of multiple jazz clubs hosting late-night gigs along Frenchmen Street. When the music switched to '80s covers, indicating they'd returned to the Quarter, he knew they were close to home.

"I really love the place you picked out. It's such a nice walk from the Scratchy Dog. Too bad we haven't been able to spend more time here."

She hugged his arm tightly to her body. "Though I am worried about the girls, walking with you through the city at night is one of my favorite parts of the day. I get you all to myself."

He kissed her wavy black hair. "We do seem to get pulled into hell's dramas quite frequently."

She looked up at him. Her dark-brown eyes made his heart beat just a little faster. "I don't just mean the paranormal aspect of our relationship. You know how much I love our dogs, but we need more time for only the two of us."

"I never thought I'd hear you put me ahead of Cheesecake."

She snuggled her head back against his shoulder. "I don't see love as a competition."

"I guess I'm not very good at being romantic."

Kendell stopped walking and pulled him into her arms. "I've had my fair share of passionate boyfriends. Romance is like the first scent of a freshly cut rose—magical and enticing. Being partners is closer to tending a garden. It's dirty and sweaty—and not always fun. A cut flower is a lovely gesture, but it will wither away. Taking care of plants, however, proves to be a new experience each time you enter the garden. Boyfriends have always been short term for me, but you've got me stuck to you forever." She hugged him tightly, and he wondered where she found the strength after the long night of playing onstage.

"Maybe the dogs should sleep in the living room tonight."

MYLES WAS up early the next morning. The night of passion proved more invigorating than tiring for him. He snuck out of the bed, hoping not to disturb Kendell. The way she cuddled the oversized pillow to her face made him wish they could turn their backs on hell. The devil didn't have the right to even be tempted by such an angelic face.

She'd endured so much to save him, the band—everyone really—from the curse they'd stumbled into. Though Kendell wouldn't admit it, Baron Malveaux—who'd joined spirits with Lincoln Laroque to become Colin Malveaux—not so secretly had a crush on her. Now that Colin considered himself the devil, hell was the last place Myles wanted Kendell spying into.

After he finished his coffee, he picked up the small black Lhasa apso puppy and looked at the older dog on the ottoman. "It's okay, girl. I'm just taking my buddy on a little walk. Keep an eye on Kendell for me."

Cheesecake lifted her head from her paws. Now that the other two pups had found their homes with Polly and Lynn, the old girl was less protective of her remaining puppy.

Kendell emerged from the bedroom, wearing a nightshirt so short he considered putting off his meeting with the band. "We'll be fine. I promise not to cast any voodoo spells while you and the girls peer into hell."

He wondered if it was worth having her attempt to contact the baron Malveaux's family. As guardians of the third and fourth gates, they would be more likely to understand what Colin was up to, though even he wasn't sure how to reach them. Miss Fleur had died over a hundred years ago in Our Lady of Mercy convent, and her two children were also ghosts from the past.

"I won't be long," he said. "Aren't you supposed to go see Mary across the river?"

"You don't think she could contact her alternate-reality self, do you?" Kendell had an expression of concentration as if she were trying to work out a trigonometry equation in her head.

"She claimed to be a *seer*. Even with all we've been through, I'm not sure what that means. Clearly, she wasn't talking about knowing the future. I still find it confusing how her alternate self could understand our lives from her dimension. Since the Mary we know across the river is the only one you can talk to, I can't see how she'd be of any help, but that alternate version of her does watch over the first gate."

Kendell brushed by him as she headed to the kitchen. "It will give me and Cheesecake something to do, and if she can access that alternate reality, maybe her alternate self can keep an eye on you. Good luck with the band."

Out on the street, he suspected having a small dog walking at his side didn't improve his manliness, but the way Doughnut Hole swaggered along the sidewalk as though he owned the whole French Quarter made Myles proud to be the pup's escort. "You still see yourself as that hellhound who would take on any demon, don't you? Well, I guess you've earned that right."

After spending a month in hell with only the gang of women and the devil, Myles found it hard not to be distracted by every passing face. He couldn't shake the constant feeling that with just a little psychological push, he could get to know anyone down to his or her most personal detail.

At the front door of the club, he looked down at Doughnut Hole to avoid making any more eye contact than was necessary. He fished the key to the front door out of his pocket.

"Hey there, mister business owner."

Myles turned to the street and saw Charlie leaning out the driver's side of his beat-up truck.

"Knock that off. You here for a delivery?"

Charlie got out, which made the truck's suspension squeak. "Feel like giving me a hand?"

Some habits were hard to break. "You're the boss."

"Bullshit. I know Kendell finally got you to add your name to the deed. Besides, I may manage the bar, but you stopped being junior to me the minute we quit the club on Bourbon Street."

Myles pushed open the door made of weathered wood and glass. He still wasn't sure Papa Ghede's gift of the establishment wasn't just some supernatural joke. "She said either I sign my name or she'd tear up the deed. I couldn't risk a war with the afterlife. Honestly, this place feels more like a clubhouse than a business. And you know we'd be lost without you."

"Yeah, yeah. Save it for my bonus. What brings you here so early in the morning? Or do I even want to ask?"

Charlie was one of the few people who, though not directly associated with the paranormal adventures, was always there to help. "I need to check in on that parallel dimension. The band should be along shortly to do the same."

"Naturally." Charlie set the case of Captain Morgan on the bar as casually as if Myles was talking about a burned-out light bulb that needed replacing.

Myles took the piece of chalk used for listing the drink specials and drew the veve Kendell had created for the second gate on the stage. "Things might get a little paranormal around here."

"Don't they always?" Charlie grabbed a bottle of rum out of the case. "You need something for your hideaway?"

"Not this time. Besides, the loas aren't fans of the cheap stuff."

"Tourists aren't picky, but you might have a point. Who

do I talk to about stocking some expensive liquor for our supernatural VIPs?"

Myles couldn't give a damn about the business's finances, and he knew neither would Kendell. "We put you in charge for a reason. Do what you think is best for the club. When the band gets here, let them know I'm out back."

Doughnut Hole had already found a sunny spot in the courtyard, but when he saw Myles, he jumped up as though he'd been called to attention.

"It's okay, boy. I'm not planning on needing your hellhound protection."

But seeing the little dude made Myles put off his chore for the moment. With no one around to judge his childlike behavior, he got down on the brick-covered ground and rolled around with the puppy.

"Our fearless leader," said a familiar voice.

He didn't know how long Polly and the band had been standing in the doorway, laughing at him. He got up and tried to look dignified. "Well, if some people would be on time... screw it. I'd play with my puppy all day. I don't even care if that makes me less masculine."

Lynn was the first to get on the ground to join Cupcake in greeting Doughnut Hole. "I don't think there's anything sexier than a guy who's not afraid to show his love for dogs. Besides, we're practically your sisters. You don't have to play the macho male with us."

Polly drew the fifth veve on the bar with the chalk Myles had tossed onto it. "So how do we do this thing? I know Baron Samedi said we could use the gates to look in on hell, but he seemed to be a little short on details."

Myles jumped over the counter and pulled out a bottle of absinthe and one of cognac. "Find the guitar pick that Kendell offered as tribute should Colin pass your test. I offered a Sazerac. Put the tribute on the veve. From there, your guess is as good as mine."

Myles seldom had time to make fancy drinks at the bar. Rum and Coke was about as complicated as it got most nights. He pulled out the chilled old-fashioned glass and rinsed the inside with absinthe. By the time he had the remaining ingredients ready to be strained into the prepared glass, the women in the next room had stopped talking—a sure sign they were accessing their gate to hell.

Doughnut Hole sat at attention on the other side of the bar, wagging his tail like an expectant customer.

"This isn't for you, boy." Myles set the prepared drink on the middle of the veve. To re-create the gate, he focused on the memory of being in hell and sitting at the speakeasy while Kendell performed her magic. As it came into existence, instead of the calm night he remembered, rain was cascading down the four roofs into the courtyard. Protected by the shutters, he felt as if he were serving the drink from under a waterfall. Doughnut Hole remained where he was, completely dry and still wagging his tail.

"So far, this is telling me exactly nothing. I already knew Colin was sent back in time a few hours to suffer the hurricane again."

Doughnut Hole gave him a firm bark.

Myles suspected the dog was right. He was missing something. Looking up into the swirling rain, he spotted debris that had been caught up in the maelstrom. "That's not right. Hurricanes pick up all kinds of stuff. Everything up there looks far too uniform in size."

A change in the winds brought the cloud of refuse down toward the courtyard. Instead of thousands of red plastic cups pummeling him, however, bats filled the space above his makeshift bar.

The winged rodents landed and hung upside down from the lifted shutters that acted as a roof over the speakeasy. Their eyes turned from beady black to glowing red.

Myles flicked the Sazerac against the brick wall, breaking the glass and the spell. "Come on, boy. We have to stop the band from staring too long into their gate."

The pup was already barking at his sisters before Myles could get over the bar counter.

"Cut the connection!" Myles yelled from the courtyard. "Colin is using his bats to keep an eye on the gates." He rushed into the club and saw the four women sitting around the veve, stunned. "Is everyone okay?"

Polly took a couple of deep breaths. "Yeah, but I never knew I had such a fear of bats. They were outside the club, beating on the window. Another couple of minutes, and they'd have broken the glass."

He sat on the edge of the stage and lifted Doughnut Hole to join his sisters, who were cuddled next to the band members. "The information that Colin has gained even more control of hell's creatures wasn't what I'd hoped to learn. Did any of you notice anything useful?"

"It's raining again," Minerva said.

Lynn snuggled Cupcake tightly to her side. "So he hasn't learned anything meaningful. Sanguine said her grandmother would only move time forward if he learned what she was trying to teach."

Myles didn't see how that obvious conclusion was much help. "Any insight into Sanguine?"

The four women sat silently around their veve.

"Me neither," Myles said.

Polly set Muffin Top aside. "I respect Kendell's fear of us getting sucked back into hell, but this weakness is like having voodoo mono. No matter how much sleep I get, I'm always ready for a nap."

Scraper leaned back against the wall. "When Polly complains about not having any energy, we'd all better worry."

"What are you suggesting?" Myles asked.

"You need to connect to us the way you did in hell. Even if you can't talk to Sanguine, maybe you can figure out a way to turn off the psychic spigot."

He hated acting without consulting Kendell, but he also didn't want to fight with her over something he knew he had to do. "We all need to lie on the stage with our heads pressed against each other. Don't fall asleep. I can bind us together again, but if things get dangerous, I'm relying on the puppies to distract us. If you hear them barking, work your attention back to this stage. I just want to get a look at what's going on."

Polly was the first to lie down on the gray-painted plywood stage. "Just get this thing out of me. If what Kendell felt while connected to the curse is anything like being hooked up to Sanguine, I'll never again give her shit about that golden guitar pick. I can't imagine how she stayed sane."

Myles didn't have the heart to tell Polly that Sanguine was practically a saint compared to Baron Malveaux. The women's hair flowed around his head. Normally, so many women making themselves open to him would have been unbearably nerve-racking, but Lynn was right—they were closer to sisters to him than anyone he had known.

He opened his soul to them. Next, he focused on Sanguine, feeling a bit like a member of a bomb-disposal unit heading into a minefield. The women weren't the issue. Taking a second journey to the outskirts of hell, however, seemed a little too much like literally tempting the devil.

Protecting the women's spirits felt a lot like holding Doughnut Hole. The little dude had unequivocal trust in Myles's strength. That level of responsibility for another's love wasn't something he'd ever experienced from another living being, not even Kendell. She was a strong spirit who would accept his help but never let herself become dependent. The band, however, was so sapped of strength that they nestled into his spirit like little girls falling asleep against their father's chest. The impression was one he knew he'd need to keep to himself.

Hell's doors were closed. The alternate reality that resembled life was no more than a dream—a dream in which Sanguine ruled. Her spirit was out there somewhere in the bayous she called home. He saw his connection to her as a belaying rope that kept her from slipping off the cliff of life. The band's exhaustion was caused by each woman holding onto the end of Myles's spiritual rope to ensure he didn't slip out of their grasp and go over the edge into hell.

They were doing the work. He was merely the conduit. As was frequently the case when Myles was involved in some dangerous physical endeavor, he didn't realize the risks until someone else also had their life on the line.

Doughnut Hole nudged Myles's hand with his wet nose, breaking the connection Myles had to the women.

---

2

*S*anguine sat on a limb of a live oak that overlooked Bayou Saint John. Wind teased the tips of her five-foot-long wings. She wasn't impressed with the well-manicured waterway, but being within the city limits, it at least gave her a taste of home. Her two alligators —Left and Right—lounged on the freshly cut grass below the tree. They were profoundly lazy creatures without a worry in hell. She envied them.

She wasn't ready to face Colin. He'd had months to learn how to control his surroundings. The time with Kendell and her gang of idiots had only served to show Sanguine how far their adversary had progressed.

She swung her feet like a little girl who didn't want to come in for dinner. The action brushed her feather tips against her reptilian companions, who looked up at her in displeasure. Even though they were physical and she merely spirit, she'd managed to teach them to respond to every one of her directions, even unintentional ones. "Sorry. You know, you two could try to do some work."

They both returned to their contemplation of the water.

Sitting around in the trees like some overly emotional woodland fairy wasn't getting her any closer to killing Colin. She pulled out the sword she kept sheathed at her side. The blue metal shone in the early morning light. To prove its uselessness, she swung it through the tree as if chopping it down with one blow. Not a single leaf rustled. She aimed the blade at the water. Her two companions promptly got up from their grassy bed and tromped to the edge of the bayou. At least the animals obeyed. Like a sword of justice, whatever she pointed at, her animal companions would attack.

She returned the blade to its sheath. *I might not be able to interact with Colin physically yet, but I can direct the animals to do my bidding. So I've got that going for me.*

Time was the real problem. Her grandmother might conjure up a dimensional hurricane as easily as she would mix up a batch of pralines, but the old swamp witch had neglected to give Sanguine the recipe. It was a power Sanguine understood, yet turning the swirling winds backward—and thus turning back time—still had the young swamp witch stumped.

She spread her wings and hopped off the limb. Her feet settled to the ground with all the gentleness of a leaf drifting on a windless fall day. A mosquito buzzed her face. By the time she thought about swatting it away, it had zigzagged off to her left. She stared at the retreating insect until it was out of sight. "You knew exactly which hand I was going to raise and which direction it would swish through the air."

She summoned the bug back to her. No matter which way she looked, the insect parried her move like a fencing opponent. "You can't be that good. That brain of yours is too small for such advanced calculations."

As a test, she stood perfectly still, as only a spirit not burdened with a body could do. By letting her attention wander, she was able to see life from the perspective of the mosquito. The myriad of lenses the insect used didn't display a 180-degree view as she'd been taught in school. The bug could see the future and the past. Like a puppeteer, Sanguine directed her body to move a finger. Before she made the movement, the lens directly ahead of the mosquito displayed the action. As the thought of moving her finger became a reality, the bug switched its focus from the future to the present. Even when the finger had resumed its natural position, she could still see it extended in the final insect view screen. Every movement she made was displayed across time as if it were a film of events in which the projector wasn't simply focusing through a small lens but showing multiple frames at the same time.

"So you can see the future and the past even though time is standing still here in hell." She tried to work out what that meant to her current situation. "To see the future, you'd have to live in the past. In your case, it must be only a fraction of a second, but the concept would hold true no matter the length of time."

Before she mentally released the bug, the little insect had laid out its escape vector.

Sanguine hunched her wings higher up her shoulders so she could sit by the water's edge. Though her two gator companions couldn't have cared less about what she had to say, at least they didn't offer unwanted advice like Kendell's meddlesome friends.

"Colin is stuck in time, but I'm not. I chose to stay in this moment because it's closer to when he is. Every second I don't have to turn back makes it easier to reach him. But what will I see if I do go back in time?"

Left didn't bother looking up, and Right snapped at a bug that had landed on his snout.

"Like that mosquito, I should be able to see Colin's future, even if he doesn't have one based on time moving. I've always assumed he would die in that moment he's stuck in. He will if I have anything to say about it. But our little friend was able to see my movements independent of time's passage."

Right grew tired of the conversation and crawled into the water without fully standing on his stubby legs.

"You're just not interested in science at all, are you?"

Left turned his big green eye to her and blinked with his multiple eyelids.

"Good point, Lefty. I wouldn't *know* the future—I'd only see what's about to happen in the direction I'm looking. After all, mosquitos can be killed if they're not looking at what's coming at them. You can be quite wise for a gator."

She could see the trap. Thinking she knew more than she actually did would make her vulnerable. No matter how fast she turned her head or how far ahead she could see in time, there would always be the danger of the hand coming around behind her and squishing her.

"I'm getting ahead of myself, aren't I? Seeing into the future requires multiple-lens eyes and a trip back in time. Of course, being spirit and not animal, I can at least accomplish one of those tasks. Don't freak out on me."

She closed her eyes and imagined seeing different perspectives on time like her mosquito mentor. Having eyes that took up half her face didn't seem like a means of passing inconspicuously, but turning her light-blue irises into multiple lenses might make them look like cut-glass jewels.

When she opened her eyes and looked at Left, she could see he was about to fall asleep.

～

COLIN MALVEAUX STORMED around the French Quarter like the hurricane that had just passed. The source of his ire wasn't losing, once again, to the sexy little witchy guitarist. As a businessman, he'd suffered his fair share of setbacks. The one thing he was certain of was that she would be back for another of their life-or-death chess matches.

The rain, however, which he had been so relieved to be rid of, once again soaked everything it touched. "You are not playing fair, old witch! Once something is learned, it can't be unlearned. Just because I reject what you taught me, that doesn't make it right for you to turn back time."

Arguing with a hurricane only made his throat hurt. Agnes Delarosa was dead. The part of her that made up

Colin's hell couldn't be reasoned with, no matter how hard he tried. "Try this, witch."

He waved his hand toward the storm. A cloud of bats circled overhead, blackening the sky and creating a living umbrella. With the flapping of their wings, they managed to divert the rain for a hundred-foot radius around him.

But even the rain and having the old witch turn the hands of time back a few hours wasn't what made every animal other than the bats steer clear of Colin. Hell was no longer his alone. He had felt the change even before being confronted with the voodoo totem that had imprisoned the side of him known as Baron Malveaux. With the hated African sculpture taking up residence in Delphine de Galpion's Scratch and Sniff perfumery, her back room full of Marie Laveau's voodoo journals was inaccessible. He hadn't just lost a battle—the deck had been reshuffled, and he was no longer assured of being dealt a winning hand.

Then there were the animals. Before Kendell and her band of miscreants invaded his hell, every living creature responded to him as the god that he was. Battling Sanguine for control of his pets had been a worthy contest. But now that the meddlesome kids had left, hell's animals seemed to think they'd been set free. The bats, of course, still obeyed Colin without reserve, as did the rats and most varieties of scurrying insect, but any creature heavier than a pound treated him like an equal.

His conclusion was inescapable. "I'm not alone. Somehow, that young swamp witch has retained power in my hell."

He sat at the doors of Saint Louis Cathedral to consider

his resources. Scratch and Sniff was out, not that there was much left in the establishment. The fire wraiths he'd saved from Delphine's curio cabinets had been returned to their totems, which he kept in his penthouse office. Other than his fiery pets, he'd found little of interest in the shop.

According to his bat spies, his old office at New Orleans Bank and Trust was more than one of the seven gates of hell. Kendell and her gang had turned it into a gate between his hell and her reality. At one time, as Baron Malveaux, it had been Colin's seat of power, but without Baron Samedi's cane, the office was just another artfully decorated room when it came to its usefulness.

A line of bats stretched over the horizon. The old swamp witch's lair hadn't been of much use even when the old woman had been alive. Now that her granddaughter—the source of his disquiet—had inherited the realm, he considered making the long journey, though he doubted she would be holed up, waiting for him. Any worthy adversary would take the initiative and not wait for their opponent to catch up.

As for the remaining gates between life and hell, he had his bats to inform him if anything changed. So far, with the momentary exception, each location was as dank and empty as it had been when he first found himself in hell. Having been a loa of the dead, he knew what was expected. He was to be a good little boy, do his lessons, and present himself to the gate guardians like some stupid altar boy looking for absolution.

"Did they really think I was that foolish?"

He longed to return to his penthouse office. Memories

of taking on fellow businessmen and crushing their achievements to dust gave him a feeling of satisfaction, but even with time standing still, he couldn't face living in the past.

What he needed was power, and lacking control over humans, he'd turned to animals. Now that they too were rebelling, he would distill his desire to the most basic elements.

He stood, brushed the dust from the church off his pants, and turned to the abandoned World Trade Center. His voodoo totems, absconded from Delphine's shop, still stood guard at the four wings of the building like gargoyles. The old swamp witch had made a tactical error in sending him back into the hurricane. Power from the storm would be building up in the strangely shaped structure exactly as intended by the designers, but instead of using the electricity to keep the vaults that housed Luther Noire's collected paranormal items from gaining strength, he'd use the totems to redirect the power and release his fury—just as he had when he'd busted in on the little game Kendell and her friends had been playing to create their gates.

"Power is power, no matter the form. Once I have control of it, I can set my trap."

With every step toward the building on the river, he felt his confidence returning. He'd been a fool for letting self-doubt infect his thoughts.

He looked up beyond the bats overhead. "Thank you for the lesson, old witch, though I doubt it's the one you meant to teach me."

The lobby of the World Trade Center lit up as he walked

through the doors. In some parallel dimension, Luther Noire would be keeping an eye on his repository. It grated on Colin's nerves that he had to ask permission to enter the building beyond the lobby. He smiled at his irritation. "Item number one: disable Luther's hold on *my* building."

He lifted the phone from the guard desk and punched in 6-6-6. "Let me up."

The man's irascibility came through loud and clear. "Why?"

Colin did his best not to release his anger. *There will be time for that later. Right now, I need determination.* "I thought I'd collect my possessions."

There was silence from the other end. Colin knew Luther would be considering how to lay claim to Marie Laveau's voodoo totems, but as the wooden sculptures weren't in Luther's dimension, and Colin was the only person in hell, Luther didn't have many choices.

"Make it quick," Luther said.

A light came on over the middle elevator. *I'll take as much devil-damned time as I want, you fat fuck.* Colin closed his eyes in self-loathing at the unintended mental release of anger. Power was power, and he didn't want to release even a sentence's worth of it until he had it focused like a laser beam against his true enemies.

The elevator opened to the circular room at the top of the building. Everything was just as Colin had left it. He found the consistency reassuring. If he kicked something over, it would stay that way. If he left a book open to a specific page, nothing would change until he returned to resume his reading.

He walked past the conference table with Marie's journals still open to the spells he'd used to release the energy from the totems. Four of the wooden heads looked out the windows at their brethren stuck outside in the storm. He thought of his earlier attempt to spin the room like a giant turbine and use the totems to direct the supernatural energy, gathered from Luther's little playthings, out into the paranormal stream. In retrospect, that strategy seemed like child's play. Colin needed to direct that power, not simply release it like a kid throwing a temper tantrum.

The door to the main control room behind the circular stage stood open. To combat Kendell, all he'd needed was to release the building's magical lightning bolts. Now he would have to figure out what all the dials, levers, and gauges were meant to accomplish. The main gauge, which displayed the building's current charge, had pointed to zero when he'd last left the room. Without electricity provided by the city or a storm to energize the structure's grid, he'd drained the ample supply without thinking. The witch's mistake was paying off. The gauge now read 25 percent. He once again had power at his command.

3

*M*yles kept the cane he'd received from Papa Ghede locked away in a gun safe. He hated guns and everything associated with them. The gray-painted steel safe in the back of his closet didn't provide him any comfort, but at least no one would be stealing the magic stick.

Papa Ghede had said Myles needed to learn how to use the cane that had belonged to Baron Samedi. Though the staff had always been meant for him, even before he was born, Myles couldn't hold it without feeling the energy of Baron Malveaux. Too many bad memories accompanied removal of the cane from the locker.

"Why are you staring at that thing?" Kendell always seemed to know when he was facing a crisis.

He closed the closet door, wishing it were as easy to ignore his thoughts. "Did you learn anything from Mary?"

She shot him the familiar look that said, *You're not getting out of this that easily.* "We had a pleasant lunch. Now that her clan owns the land along the batture, they aren't as paranoid of strangers as they used to be. She let me take her out to that steakhouse next to the ferry, even though she was uncomfortable being around people her family begs from. I just wanted to do something nice as a thank-you for all she's done for us. I guess I've still got a lot to learn about people."

Though he enjoyed the recap of her day, that hadn't been the point of her trip across the river. "How did she take the news that there's an alternate-reality version of herself that owns that whole piece of land?"

"About as you'd expect. Everyone believes there's an alternate-reality version of themselves that's a king or a celebrity or whatever. I don't think she even stopped eating her gumbo at the news. Honestly, she seemed more interested in explaining to me why the dish was so bland."

As he'd feared, Kendell hadn't found some magical alternative to the cane locked in his closet. "So no secret insight into what Colin's up to?"

"Nope. How did things go at the Scratchy Dog?"

From inside the closed closet, behind the coats in the locked gun cabinet, the cane called to him. "A strikeout would have been preferable. Colin knew we were peeking into his world. Those bats of his seemed to have experienced a population explosion. I joined souls with the band to see what we're up against." He gave her a moment to digest the information. From the expressions of shocked anger and then acceptance, he knew she was conducting his argument for him far better than he'd have done.

"What did you learn?"

"Sanguine isn't just using the band's psychic energy. We're holding her to life, and that line is slipping."

Kendell pointed at the closed closet. "Something tells me that's why you were considering opening that gun locker."

He opened the door, feeling like he was revealing a hidden porn collection. "We can't talk to Sanguine as she's cut off in hell, but we also can't sit by and let her drain the band until they too become comatose. For one thing, we don't have that much couch space. And if we can't hold onto Sanguine, we'll lose her to Colin's domain."

Kendell crossed her arms. "That's why you wanted to know about Mary before telling me about the cane. You were hoping we could talk to her over one of the gates. As there's a version of Mary who isn't part of our dimension, you were grasping at the last straw."

"Something like that. Only we don't need to just talk to Sanguine."

He barely got his sentence out before she objected. "We are not taking the girls back into hell."

"Agreed. In their condition, they might not even make the trip. But that's all academic because we can't enter the gates, only guard them."

She eased up on her defiant stance. "So what's your idea?"

"We're going to have to sneak in the back door. Just you and me—no other people, no dogs, no magic. Colin has his realm staked out. He'll notice any big changes like us driving Minerva's VW bus into hell like last time. However, he is stuck in a single moment. That leaves us a lot of time to enter and figure out how to sync up with Sanguine."

"But Baron Samedi closed the seventh gate of Guinee."

Myles opened the gun cabinet. "His seventh gate was never between hell and Guinee. When he got sucked into Agnes Delarosa's hurricane with Colin, Baron Samedi's spirit punched a hole between the two realms. Even though having him return to Guinee closed the hole, that passage still exists. It's like one of those old brick walls you see in the Quarter where at one time a window opening was bricked in. You can still see the outline of what was there. With this cane, I should be able to knock out just enough of those metaphorical bricks to let us pass."

He could see her objections coming. He'd argued most of them himself.

"But we'd have to pass through Guinee, and Baron Samedi can't help us. He's back at his guard station. Papa Ghede made it sound like there would be a full-on revolt from Baron Kriminel if that balance of power isn't maintained."

Myles removed the cane. "That's why it's up to us."

"You're not just talking about us making another spiritual journey, are you? You want us to bodily walk into Guinee. The living aren't supposed to wander the streets of the dead."

The power of the cane radiated in Myles's hand. "My plan gets worse. Remember how Baron Samedi couldn't leave the bank office, and how his time there took a toll on him? If I'm right, I'll have to stand at the opening so you can pass. If I got stuck on the other side, I would be in the same predicament Baron Samedi was in. That means you'll be alone to find Sanguine. So long as Colin remains in her version of the past, we should be okay."

"Right. I'll just have to find her in all of New Orleans and the swamp she calls home. And on foot no less."

"My hope is that she'll find you. She has been sucking up a lot of energy. Her skills, even before this adventure, were with understanding animals. My guess is she's using the animals to keep a watchful eye on everything that's happening in hell. She did a pretty good job at talking those snakes off of your legs."

Kendell shivered. "Don't remind me. What if she doesn't want to leave? She can be pretty obstinate when she wants to be."

He refrained from making the comparison with Kendell. "She wouldn't be staying there if she didn't have a plan."

"We *had* a plan. Remember? Building those seven gates wasn't just a day at the beach, making sandcastles."

"Tell it to Sanguine."

SNEAKING through a war zone involving the loas of the dead in order to gain access to hell sounded like a really bad idea to Kendell, but she didn't have a better one. They hadn't yet discussed Myles's progress with the cane. She knew he stayed up nights playing with the damn thing in secret. Not that she blamed him. When a lord of the afterlife told someone to learn how to use their magic for the battle ahead, that person didn't have much choice but to listen.

"So how do we get to Guinee, and once there, what do you expect we'll find?"

His hand on top of the staff glowed green from the stone nestled under the silver skull handle of the walking stick. "We're using a walking cane, so we get to Guinee by walking. I'm just hoping all hell isn't breaking loose—literally or figuratively—when we arrive."

She put her hand around his arm as if he were escorting her into a fashionable party. "Let's get on with it."

Stepping from one reality to the other was as easy as walking from the hallway to the living room—only this living room resembled Basin Street of the Storyville era. Gaslights lit the cobblestone street and the entrance of every building. Music from tinny pianos mixed with women's laughter. Dust kicked up from the passing horse carts hung in the humid air.

"I can't quite place the smell," Myles said. "It's kind of a combination of horse manure, sulfur, and really bad perfume."

"You're not helping. At least we're not in the middle of a post-apocalypse war. This sure isn't what I expected."

He pointed to a sign over the nearest building. Gate Number One. In the dim light, it would have been unreadable had it not been written in big red letters. "No one ever accused the loas of subtlety."

"Should we enter?" Kendell asked.

With her hand still around his arm, he guided her to the wooden walkway that connected the buildings. "We're not trying to open the gates to the *deep waters*, so we should be safe trying to find Baron Samedi without the ritual of entering every gate in order."

As they passed the building, Kendell looked in the rippled-glass window. To her astonishment, people were drinking and dancing like some 1800s version of Bourbon Street. "I don't get it. I thought the dead were just supposed to pass through Guinee. What are all these people doing here?"

"Having fun apparently. Baron Malveaux kept his women prisoners in Guinee. Maybe this isn't just a bus station like we thought."

She could see the appeal of not wanting to let go of the life she'd spent so long building. If she'd died as these people had, she couldn't imagine carrying on without those she loved. "What about the battle between the loas of the dead?"

Myles nodded toward the door below the Gate Number Two sign. "Let's poke our noses in. Guede Nibo was the nicest of all the loas when I was possessed by Baron Malveaux. Plus, he was taken in by Baron Samedi when he first got here, so hopefully he'll be willing to fill us in on what's going on."

The rough-hewn wooden bar, unfinished floor, and general grungy appearance of the place more properly fit a Hollywood Western than a realm of the dead.

"What the hell?" Kendell pointed at the table in the back of the establishment, where Baron Samedi was playing cards with another loa of the dead.

"You two aren't supposed to be here."

Kendell saw Guede Nibo serving drinks behind the bar.

Myles escorted her to a barstool in front of the loa. "We need to talk to Baron Samedi. There's trouble in hell."

Nibo leaned over the bar conspiratorially. "When is there not trouble in hell? My baron is playing for this establishment at the moment. I wouldn't want to disturb him. The competition is down to the final two."

"I don't understand," Kendell said.

"What's to understand? You don't have betting in the world you come from? Things sure have changed."

"Of course we have gambling," she said. "Is this what all the commotion was about regarding a war between the loas for control of Guinee? A simple game of cards?"

"Nothing simple about it. How would you propose we settle our conflicts? A physical altercation proves nothing other than who's stronger, and driving one of us from Guinee would leave a gate unattended. Trust me, it's enough work just looking after this place. Having to run two gates would run any loa ragged."

Slowly, she began to see the brilliance of their means of settling conflict. "But if one of them loses yet doesn't want to run the other club, what are the stakes?"

"Control takes many forms, but I doubt you've crossed over to the land of the dead to learn about our gambling habits. Since I can tell you aren't among the dead, others will notice too. You'd best conduct your business as fast as you can."

Myles lifted his cane so Guede Nibo could see it. "We're just passing through, but our escape lies within Baron Samedi's seventh gate."

"I see. Then you'd better hope he wins this game against

Baron Kriminel. Keep to the shadows. If Kriminel knows you're here, you might have a rough time getting out. Leave before Baron Samedi gets up from the table."

Kendell hadn't been a fan of cards since the night a former boyfriend had conned her into a game of strip poker. She barely knew the rules and was lost when it came to identifying the winning hand. From the expressions and gestures of the patrons standing behind the two contestants, however, it wasn't hard to figure out who was winning.

Baron Samedi laid down his hand with a look of triumph.

Kriminel threw his cards on the table with such force that they skidded off to the floor. "You win this round, but we're just getting started."

"As the winner," Baron Samedi said, "I call the next round—my club in an hour. I have something to attend to."

Myles hustled Kendell out of the club before they heard the wooden chair legs scrape along the unfinished floor. They hurried into the dark alley beside the building.

A prostitute who'd been lingering by the door followed them out as if they were potential clients. She checked the street before joining them in the alley. "Take me with you. I'm not supposed to be dead. This is all a horrible mistake. They're holding me against my will."

Though Kendell's natural urge was to help the frightened woman, she knew the truth of what she was about to say. "You don't want to end up where we're headed. There are places far worse than purgatory."

The shadow of a man darkened the narrow passage,

causing the woman to flee down the alley away from the street.

"As Nibo said, you don't belong here."

Kendell let out a deep breath, realizing it was Baron Samedi. "Sanguine's soul got left behind in hell. We can't reach her any other way."

"Now that you're here, I suppose it would be pointless arguing with you."

Myles stood the cane in front of him. "You were able to get from hell back to Guinee with this staff. My plan depends on that passage working both ways."

"Come with me. We'll keep to the alleyways and sneak in the kitchen to the seventh gate. Don't let anyone see you."

Kendell didn't want to speculate on what dangers were involved as a living human caught in the afterlife. From the way Baron Samedi stuck to the shadows and guided them through the maze of back passages, she guessed the danger wasn't only to her and Myles.

Finally, the dark loa escorted them between two buildings with the main street they'd started on at the end of the passage. He opened a service door and rushed them inside. "I realize that was the long way down the street, but the cloak and dagger was necessary. If these souls realized there was a way from Guinee back to life, we could have an uprising."

Kendell didn't have the courage to tell him about the prostitute. Bracing herself for another journey to hell seemed like enough stress for one day.

Instead of entering the saloon, Baron Samedi directed them up a narrow stairway at the back of the building.

"Patrons use the main staircase to the second floor. This one's reserved for house cleaning, so it doesn't get much use at this time of day. You should be okay so long as no one sees Myles standing guard."

Kendell thought about being trapped alone in hell, and her legs felt as though all the muscles had turned to pudding. She wondered if she'd be able to stand upright, let alone wander the realm searching for her friend. "I doubt Sanguine is going to be waiting at the door. She might not be that easy to find. What happens if the trip takes longer than just a few minutes?"

"Since time isn't passing in the witch's hell, it won't pass here either. Don't let time move, and you'll be fine." He paused at the top of the stairs. "The door will only open to the instant you left hell. If your intent is to move through time in hell to pursue Colin Malveaux, the gate will do you no good."

Myles gripped the cane below the silver skull. "Kendell just needs to convince Sanguine to return to her body."

Baron Samedi motioned to a door at the end of the hallway. "From what I saw of her, you'll have your work cut out convincing her of anything." He opened the door to a dusty broom closet that stank of cleaning solvents. "This is what anyone in Guinee would see. When I close the door, rap on it with the cane and open it again. You'll see the bank office. Myles will have to stand guard on this side of the door until you return. We can't risk any of our charges wandering into the wrong room."

Kendell couldn't contain her curiosity. "I assume this is a brothel, but where do your souls go to find the *deep waters*?"

He waved his hand at the doors that lined the hallway. "These rooms, of course. The sooner you go, the less danger of being caught."

Myles quietly struck the door. "Don't let Sanguine talk you into some foolhardy adventure. Drag her by the hair if you have to, but get her back to this gate. We know Colin is back in time relative to when we left. Since I don't remember opening this door to you, I have to believe we'd be in deep voodoo if you went back in time."

She kissed him on the cheek. "I'll be back before you know it."

4

"*L*ike flying isn't confusing enough," Sanguine muttered to the mosquito flying point.

Seeing the past, present, and future while flapping her wings enough to prevent falling made Sanguine dizzy. Each time she changed where she was looking, she saw herself plowing headfirst into the scenery. Banking away from the impending collision, however, only changed what she was about to hit.

Her mosquito companions were of little help. If she could just land and see life through their eyes, maybe she could make some sense out of the multitime perspective, but they were insistent the only way to learn was to do, not observe. Besides, her awareness of them only extended to when she could see them. With them being so small, if she didn't keep pace, they were out of sight within a few feet. The only answer had been to fly with them.

"I fucking hate you bugs." Though animals had been her

passion while learning about Wicca, entomology had always seemed a little too nerdy. Plus, she'd had enough bloodsucking boyfriends to know when she was being played. "Fly in a damn straight line!"

She felt their reluctance, but one by one, the little insects formed up in a squadron she could follow. As her eyes settled on the single direction, the myriad of futures and pasts reduced to the New Orleans Bank and Trust straight ahead. Though the insects only had to deal with fractions of a second, Sanguine's perceptions of past and future lengthened the longer she stared in one direction.

"Damn it, Kendell!" She saw her friend walking out the front door of the establishment in five minutes. Just enough time to figure out an argument that would make Kendell scurry back home where she belonged.

However, instead of the bugs remaining focused on the path ahead, they became quite excited about the possibility of someone new to drink. The insect melee made Sanguine lose her concentration so thoroughly that she followed through on her premonition of sprawling, spread-eagle, against the front door of the bank just before Kendell opened it.

Kendell opened the door and looked down at her. "I honestly didn't expect to find you this easily. What's with the wings?"

Despite being spirit and not physical, Sanguine found her reactions to solid walls not that different from when she hauled her body around—mentally, if she hit a solid object, she crumbled to the ground.

She stood and fluffed up her wings. "I needed a way to

get around more easily. I'd need to have a whole flock to carry me, and they don't like flying at night. Wings seemed like the easiest solution."

"They look good on you. Come on. Myles is holding the door open to Guinee. From there, we can reunite you with your body."

She stared at Kendell, hoping to see her turn around and walk through the bank's doors alone. "Why can't you just leave?"

The intense look from Kendell lasted way too long. "What did you do to your eyes? They look like faceted crystals."

"Must I explain everything I've been up to? Fine. I can see the past and the future. Are you happy now?"

Kendell's folding her arms and giving a look of sisterly irritation was compounded by Sanguine seeing it before it started. "Then you know I'm not going anywhere without you."

"We can debate all day about what you're going to do and what I have planned, but I can see that's not going to happen." Sanguine was bluffing. Though she could see the future, hearing what was said didn't come with her bug vision. Without the soundtrack, understanding what was about to happen was a matter of interpretation. She barely understood what she saw.

"Whatever you're up to is draining the band of their spiritual energy. That connection Myles established with you is somehow still functioning even with you cut off in hell. If you can see far enough into the past, maybe you could ask your grandmother about it."

"Doesn't work that way." The last thing Sanguine wanted was to explain what she didn't understand herself. She sat on the stone wall that encompassed the bank so her wings could fall comfortably behind her. Looking down Royal Street gave her a sense of calm. Without people, the past, present, and future were reassuringly the same.

"What is it going to take for you to come home with me?"

"Help me kill Colin Malveaux."

Sanguine didn't need to look at Kendell to predict her reaction to that request.

"We've discussed this many times," Kendell said. "Killing him doesn't accomplish anything. This whole hell your grandmother built was to isolate him from the human continuum. If he dies, his evil just gets mixed in with the rest of us, or according to your Wiccan doctrine, he gets reincarnated. Either way, it's not like we're eliminating him."

Sanguine toyed with the handle of her sword. "Killing him is only the beginning. I'm going back in time and systematically undoing every evil deed he committed—all the way back to when he stole Baron Samedi's cane at the first Mardi Gras parade. I'm going to erase him from history. That, my dear magical sister, is what *I* call a plan."

The silence behind Sanguine lasted for so long she wondered if Kendell had done the wise thing and walked back into the bank and gone home.

"Time travel isn't possible."

Sanguine was well aware of the argument, having battled the same issue when designing her plan. "Wrong. My grandmother moved Colin back in time with her hurricane. I know this isn't life. It's hell. And I know your next argument is Agnes Delarosa is the bedrock that this hell is built on, and as such, she can do whatever she wants—including breaking the natural laws like time. I didn't say it would be easy."

"She used a hurricane to move the clock backward. For all we know, he might be only a few minutes behind us. You're talking about hundreds of years and not just in one jump."

"*I said* it wouldn't be easy." Sometimes Kendell simply didn't listen.

"And what about the band? You're killing them with your little experiment. Or is that another wrong you're somehow going to go back in time and correct?"

Hurting others hadn't been part of Sanguine's plan. The women Kendell counted on could be irritating, but they had bonded with Myles and funneled their energy to her. Had it not been for that zap of spiritual electricity, Sanguine might not have realized her power in this dimension. But then, they might also be the ones preventing her from going back in time.

"I'm not asking for them to hold onto me. If I could break the connection, I would. I'll agree to stay here with you until you find a way to free them, but I'm not going back to the living while Colin still exists."

"And what about your body lying on our couch? Should I just get a big glass coffin and use it as our coffee table?"

Sarcasm was an art form, and Kendell was as sophisticated with it as a child drawing stick figures. "If it's in the way, take it back to my grandmother's cabin. No one will bother it there. I'm going *back* in time, not forward. If this works, I'll be awake by the time you get home."

"You just don't get it, do you? I love you, you idiot. Myles and the band care about you too. *That's* what's holding them to you. Your grandmother cut Colin off from all human contact, and that's why he can move back in time. No one gives a rat's ass what happens to him. You might have wings and be able to see the future, but so long as people love you, there's no way you're moving back in time. You exist. So come up with a better plan because I'm not dumping your body in some swamp."

"And what about Colin?"

She could hear Kendell stomping around the bank's porch behind her. "We just built the seven friggin' gates. He's not going anywhere."

"Unbelievable. You really think he's just going to meekly accept being confined to his cell, don't you? Or maybe you think he'll learn his lesson and approach the seven gates to prove he's changed. I keep telling you, snakes don't change."

"I expect him to try the seven gates," Kendell said. "They're the easiest way out of his incarceration."

Sanguine turned back to Kendell, even though the vision of the continued argument made her dizzy. "Suppose he does figure out how to convince Mary he appreciates old New Orleans culture. Shouldn't be that hard really—he was a part of it. You understand enough of what my grandmother built. Tell me what happens when he actually learns something."

The look of frightened acceptance on Kendell's face was

worth watching, from the buildup through the completion. "Time moves forward."

"I don't *need* to go back in time to kill him. If you're right, he'll come to me. Then once this hell has no purpose, I can do with it what I want."

"So if he shows up in our time frame, that will prove to you that he's working his way through the seven gates and he's doing what we want?"

Sanguine felt like she'd stepped into a logic trap. "It'll prove that Mary's too softhearted. Besides, it may take him years to figure out what's expected of him. A guy like that doesn't play by the rules unless he's already exhausted every other possibility."

"Hey, if he did figure out how to get through the gate, why isn't he here already?"

Sanguine clasped her fingers together. "You and I are the two sides of his cage, remember? My grandmother wouldn't let him join our time until we're ready."

"So if he shows up here, having aged noticeably, you'll agree to return with me to your body?"

She knew when she'd been had. "This is why I never debate women who've had long-term relationships. I always end up feeling like the boyfriend who never wins an argument. I'm not promising anything. And if he doesn't show up, I'm sticking to my plan."

"But you don't even know *how* to go back in time. It's not a plan if you can't do something."

Sanguine stood and spread her wings to their full ten-foot span. "I couldn't fly when I got here either or see the future. I've only been studying this realm for a few weeks.

That is why I'm so worried about Colin. He's had time. He's just not smart enough to know what to study. Yet."

"He has a physical body. You don't. There is a difference."

Kendell just didn't get it at all.

Sanguine tried again. "We make our own reality. The number-one thing we're worried about when it comes to him returning to the living is the knowledge he's gained here in hell about how to manipulate his environment."

"So what do we do? Just stand around here until your grandmother thinks we're ready? How would we know the difference between him not finding his way through the gate and us still waiting?"

Sanguine flapped her wings. "He wouldn't show up at the bank. This is the fourth gate. If we assume that he would come far enough in time to meet us in our present time once he passes the first gate, we need to get across the river."

Kendell eyed Sanguine's wings. "Must be nice to have those things. Guess I'm in for a long walk."

Seeing what was about to happen gave Sanguine the courage to try her new magic. Without saying anything, she walked up, embraced her friend, and flapped her wings until she and Kendell were well clear of the bank.

COLIN BRUSHED out his shoulder-length hair and retied it into a ponytail. The shocks of gray that formed at his temples switched to black before reaching past his ears. His age fit him like a finely tailored suit. Time didn't exist, not that he cared. He'd added the gray to his hair as a reminder of his hard-won education. The hair's length was a nod to his many frustrations.

He peered harder into the mirror. Wrinkles had formed at the corners of his eyes. "That's new."

He stood back from the full-length mirror on the back of the door to admire his appearance. His first impression was that of a survivor. The devil in his personal hell had endured the phases of injury, anger, and acceptance. Those early days had seen him on the brink of insanity, but he'd prevailed over his own weakness of spirit. Embracing his situation had opened the door to his education, but he'd come as far as he could alone.

His perfectly tailored black suit was of such a high thread count that not a stitch could be detected even under a magnifying glass. The creases in his pants and jacket redefined the term *sharp-dressed man*. He opened the jacket to inspect the dark-purple paisley waistcoat and bloodred silk shirt. "A devil should look the part."

But this time, he hadn't dressed for his own pleasure. He turned back to what had been Luther Noire's personal office. The large oak desk and walls covered in bookcases suited him better than his penthouse office. The views of the lifeless city from his former command post in the Central Business District had grown depressing. He didn't need the reminder that there was no one to dominate. Luther's hermit-like existence had created the perfect environment for Colin to conduct his studies.

He smiled at the iron cane that leaned in the corner. His leg still ached when he made a miscalculation, but he'd surpassed the need for the crutch—mentally and physically.

He put on his top hat and floor-length overcoat. "It's time."

The elevator opened before he left the office and closed just after he went through. Like every other simple mechanical device in hell, the machinery responded to the devil's wishes without being told.

He walked into the circular central hub of the city. What had been a restaurant was now filled with control stations brought in from every city utility. The view down Canal Street had become one of his favorites. Streetcars clanged their way along the brightly lit thoroughfare like some aficionado's expensive electric toy train. With no one to drive or ride the restored trollies, they remained clean and unmolested. He watched one of the antique red-and-yellow streetcars until it disappeared on its way to City Park.

Though watching the city from his rooftop perch was an enjoyable pastime, he had work to do. He turned from the empty French Quarter to the river. With a wave of his hand, the hurricane-proof sliding door opened to the rooftop observation deck. He stepped out into the moonlit night, marveling at how much energy it had taken to move the hands of time. In some other dimension, Luther Noire would be cussing up a storm at his depleted paranormal objects. Apparently, even magic could be drained. Colin had gotten what he wanted. The time change was only the physical manifestation of his defeat of the old swamp witch. He barely remembered her or the anger he'd so foolishly cast her way. Emotions were nothing more than wasted energy.

He pushed open the gate and walked to the edge of the building. He'd come as far as he could in this version of hell. Comfortable as his realm was, growth meant he had to move on. He spread his full-length overcoat. The light, welcome breeze grew into a microhurricane that lifted him from the roof. As with the city's mechanisms, his only directive was his desire. He sailed across the river as if he were stepping across a storm drain.

A woman in a classy but comfortable summer dress stood on the porch. Her casual way of watching him descend out of the sky reminded him of a mother waiting for her child to come in for dinner. He was expected. Her anticipation worked in his favor. His feet met the ground a good dozen yards from the plantation's front steps. *Greeting a guardian of a gate from hell to life should be done on foot.*

He approached the house with all the trepidation of a door-to-door salesman. "I would guess you know who I am."

"I've been expecting you. You're older than I thought you'd be." The woman motioned to the porch swing.

He took a seat. Having the interview outside instead of in the stately house meant that he had to earn her trust. "I've been busy. How do we proceed?"

"Convince me you're not the asshole whose actions resulted in me being homeless in your version of reality."

He looked out at the lush grounds that were so different from the neighborhood Baron Malveaux had created by forcing Mary's great-grandfather to sell his land—and the man's women into prostitution. "How does a devil stop being a devil?"

"If that's your answer, this is going to be a short conversation. 'I am what I am'? Really?"

The plantation was beautiful, but so was the historic neighborhood that had been home to generations of workers. "You represent an alternate reality where this land remained in one family. The city is smaller because of your wealth. In the world I knew, workers lived here. As time passed, musicians, artists, and writers found their inspiration on this side of the river. Family properties grew in value. You are a caring woman, so answer me this: is your family's comfort worth the sacrifice to the city?"

"So the devil would defend his actions?"

He breathed in the rich aroma of the manicured lawn and the crisp, dry air of fall. "I can smell the gumbo cooking in your kitchen. If all you used were sugar and pleasant spices to flavor the dish, it would end up tasting bland. No one understands the need for pain to open the senses like a cook. Hot pepper awakens the taste buds just as suffering has infused New Orleans jazz with soul. I won't apologize for my past. What would be the point? You're not the one who's suffered."

She sat and stared at her property and then across the river. "I can see both realities. You burned down more than you created, but something new grew out of the ashes that wouldn't have existed without the destruction. I'm not sure that justifies your sins, but that's not for me to decide."

"I wouldn't ask you to believe me, but I do love this city. Set aside for a moment the part of me that did your family wrong. As a businessman with deep pockets, I could have left New Orleans for bigger dreams. Lord knows my mother pushed me hard enough to enter politics on the national stage. I chose to remain here. Even as Baron Malveaux, I never took advantage of the underprivileged— only those rich and arrogant enough to think they could best me. Your great-grandfather was a fool, but he knew what he was getting into when he borrowed money from me."

She clasped her hands in her lap. "Perhaps it's not for me to judge another person. I accepted this role as a favor to Kendell, but I wonder now, even with her connection to you, if any person is ever in a place to condemn another to hell. If I let you through my gate, how will your life change?"

"I don't know. That's why I'm here. I've come as far as I can without the help of another."

She nodded her acceptance, but in her eyes was a tinge of sorrow. "Come inside and share a bowl of gumbo with me."

---

5

*S*anguine set Kendell down on the earthen levee. Flying was challenging enough, but doing so with a passenger in her arms played hell with Sanguine's navigation. "We can walk from here."

"That sure beat having to walk across the bridge. Now that we're here, how do we find out if Colin is as well? Yell 'Abracadabra' or something?"

"Saying his name three times might work too." Sanguine had been so busy enjoying the late-afternoon sun on her wings and talking to Kendell that she hadn't bothered focusing on the plantation ahead.

"Nice wings."

She snapped her attention to the house at hearing Colin's voice from behind the screen door.

As he stepped outside, she could see what he had planned. Though flying might have been faster, she ran at him to avoid getting her wings tangled up in the trees.

But before she could reach him, he lifted his hands to the sky. "Fly away home, little ladybug."

The crack of lightning sent her tumbling to the ground. She turned back to Kendell, praying her friend was okay, but all she could make out was the electric storm that grew in intensity from the top of the World Trade Center.

"Kendell! Run!"

A ball of electric fire erupted from the top of the building and turned the sky black as if it had burned the air itself. Sanguine's ability to see time's passage in multiple screens gave her a blinding headache. Nothing she saw made sense.

When the sky cleared, she realized the trap had been set for Kendell. She was nowhere in sight. Sanguine turned back to the porch with all her anger at the ready, but Colin too had vanished. "Fuck!" She hated swearing in front of the matronly lady who'd provided the one comforting escape in hell.

Mary fell to the porch. "I couldn't have said it better, and it's all my fault. I let him through the first gate by giving him some gumbo. I thought he'd changed."

Sanguine hurried up the stairs to comfort the distraught woman. "He's a con artist. That's why I'm here. Maybe now Kendell will finally listen. Of course, we have to save her first."

"Where do you think he's taken her?"

Sanguine knew the challenge ahead. "Not where, but when."

$\sim$

KENDELL WOKE up facedown in the dirt. Whatever had hit her had turned her lights out. Her ears were ringing, and she couldn't be sure, but it felt as though someone had turned a water hose on her. "What the hell?"

"Give it a minute. Traveling back in time is kind of a gut punch."

She rolled to her back and saw Colin towering over her. The bastard was completely dry. "Mind spreading whatever magical umbrella you have over me as well?"

He looked up in shock. "My apologies." He waved his hand at the sky, and instantly the rain stopped.

"Clever little trick, as was that lightning bolt you hit me with."

He pointed at the sky as if she was supposed to be able to see anything. "My bats keep watch over me. I'm afraid I've been alone for so long my simple human decency is a little rusty."

She struggled to sit up. "No one would ever accuse you of being decent, no matter which version of your beings you chose. Now, do you mind telling me what's going on?"

He leaned down and offered her his hand. The action looked overly stiff and staged. "I'm afraid my time reversal went a little farther back than I intended. This was my first attempt at reversing time. I'd hoped to only lose a few minutes. From the storm, I'd guess we went all the way back to the beginning of my time in hell."

Her ears were still ringing as she stood up, but at least what she saw began to make sense. "I'm pretty sure you know that's not what I was asking."

"Again, it's been some time since I carried on a polite

conversation. You'll have to forgive me if I don't pick up on your nuances."

She tried to frame her question as if she were talking to a difficult child. "Why have you kidnapped me?"

"I could ask why you tossed me into hell, but neither question seems like a good beginning to our conversation. You fascinate me, but then, you're an attractive woman, and I'm sure that doesn't come as a surprise to you." He looked at Mary's home. "I suggest we get inside. Since it's the first gate to hell, I'm sure you'll understand my reservation about breaking into this plantation house. The top of the World Trade Center is quite comfortable, but as that's my home base, I'll understand if you'd rather not accept my hospitality. I'll accept any place you choose, provided it's not one of the gates."

"How gracious of you." She wondered if he'd pick up on her sarcasm. "I have an apartment in the Quarter."

"Very well." Without asking her permission, he whisked her under his arm and jumped into the air like some supervillain. The wind currents carried them across the river.

This is getting really old fast. She worried that expressing her irritation at the presumptuous act might land her in the river.

She pointed toward the block behind the church. "I live on Orleans." As they descended out of the cloud, she continued pointing at her third-floor veranda, wishing she were returning to the home she knew. It wasn't like her to invite a devil into her home. She took comfort in the idea that somewhere in a different time and dimension,

Cheesecake and Doughnut Hole were lounging in the chair or lying by the window.

As he walked in from the balcony, he removed his long coat as if he owned the building. "Nice place." His comment didn't even come close to sounding sincere.

"Don't expect me to offer you anything to eat or drink. This isn't a social situation. I'm your prisoner, not your host."

He sat on the lounge chair by the window. At first, she considered yelling at him not to take Cheesecake's spot, but then she realized maybe the old girl might get an idea of what was going on. She never took well to having her space invaded. Kendell smiled, thinking Colin might be getting his ass bitten at that very moment and not even realize it.

"We're the last two people in this dimension. All I want to do is talk."

She considered giving him the silent treatment. As a high school student, that move had worked well for her in dealings with her parents. But she wasn't the only person at risk. Panic threatened to set in at the idea of Myles still standing guard at the gate in Guinee. The one warning Baron Samedi had given was for her not to time travel. The sooner she figured out how to placate Colin and get the hell out of his dimension, the less danger Myles would have to endure. "You did a lot of work just for a chat."

"I had some time with little else to do. You haven't been an easy person to get to know."

"Maybe that's because you have been constantly stealing my dog or possessing my boyfriend or kidnapping my band. For a businessman, your approach needs a lot of work."

He shrugged as if those indiscretions had been unavoidable. "Work and pleasure don't always mesh."

"And what do I get out of our conversation?"

He sat forward on the chair and put his elbows on his knees. "I'll help you find a way back to your reality. Snapping back in time is easier than moving forward. I've only managed a day or two at a time. I have the machinery. I just need to figure out how to pump it up."

"That sounds more like a benefit to you than me. Other than getting me home, what do you intend to do with your little time machine?"

If he was trying to suppress a grin, he was unsuccessful. "I'll still be in hell, if that's what you're asking. I'd just like to experience the effortless passing of days again."

She motioned to the ceiling-fan lights. "But you've already electrified the city. Does it mean that much to you to have natural light?"

"You'd be surprised at what you miss locked away in hell. I'd be happy to share the deprivations with you."

She could envision that Colin's slipping from deprivations to depravations was only a matter of time, something he had in abundance. "Since I don't seem to have a choice, why don't we take this one step at a time. I assume you have a topic you wish to discuss."

"I've always been fascinated by the dichotomy of good and evil. As you are a gatekeeper to hell and I'm the devil himself, we might discover some hidden truth."

"I'm not sure I'm fit to represent the good in your scenario. There's a reason we set up seven gates. No one person can carry such a burden of always making the right choice."

"And yet you don't feel the same way about evil? Ultimate good is unattainable, but true evil is easy to identify?" He spoke with the assurance of a lawyer who knew his argument inside and out and was looking for a way to trip up his opponent.

Logic and critical thinking had never been her strongest subjects in college. "I think we can both agree your actions haven't shown any redeeming qualities."

"Sometimes the greatest evolution comes out of the harshest of environments while complete satisfaction of needs can lead to weak organisms."

Begrudgingly, she finally sat on the end of the couch opposite the lounge chair. "I'm familiar with the argument. Just because people are able to struggle back from adversity, that doesn't forgive the oppressor. Life has a way of balancing the equation independent of good deeds or evil intentions."

"Fair enough," he said, "but no one is fully good or evil. Life balances that as well."

Having played the devil at Robert Johnson's crossroads, Kendell was familiar with the experience of unintentionally becoming the villain. "I can accept that even the best people aren't completely good. I doubt even someone like Gandhi or Martin Luther King would make such claims about themselves. There's a humility that accompanies the good. Evil people, however, seem to relish their depravity. As Baron Malveaux, you certainly fit that description. As Lincoln Laroque, you behaved only slightly better, but taking the devil into your spirit proved your true intent."

"So you give me no hope? Then why agree to this hell Agnes Delarosa built for me? She believed I could learn to be better than I am. Isn't that the whole point of the seven gates?"

Kendell suspected debating the devil was always a losing game. "What do you want me to tell you? Yes, I think you can be redeemed. But it has to be something you want with all of your being. Half measures, like conning Mary into letting you pass through her gate only so you can hold me prisoner, only prove your lack of sincerity."

"Nothing I told her was a lie. The New Orleans that sprouted from my deeds as bank owner is unique in its culture, music, food, and art. Say what you will about my tactics, but I take pride in what this city has become. If I had to play the devil to make it happen, well, better to have that evil isolated into one person than spread across a privileged class."

Given enough time, she knew he'd wear her down. "If you truly believe what you're saying, present yourself at the seven gates. You've already gained access to the first."

"And rely on what are, as you yourself admit, flawed human beings to judge me? Do you really think the gatekeepers you appointed will keep their personal feelings out of their decisions? Your boyfriend certainly won't."

Kendell hadn't really cared if her judges would act impartially. "Can you blame him? You have a lot of evil to atone for. Asking to be pardoned from hell isn't just about showing you've changed."

"Penance is usually assessed in years. As time doesn't pass in this realm, who's to say how long my incarceration must last?"

She was starting to feel like a parole board. "I don't have an answer for you. I suppose your reality dictates how long you'll remain here."

"You mean the old swamp witch. Maybe it was Sanguine I should have captured. Though, as she clearly thinks of herself as some avenging angel, I'd have to ask where she falls on your scale of good and evil."

Kendell didn't need to imagine Sanguine's response. She'd made it clear that Colin's only fate should be death. "I doubt your conversation with her would be as civil, or long, as ours."

"So you have one member of your panel of judges who won't forgive me and one who only wants to see me dead. Do we really need to analyze the remaining members of the judiciary? You must see the impossibility of me passing through the gates, just as I do."

The gates had been meant as a way to control Colin. So long as he thought he could gain forgiveness, he might avoid trying to break down the walls of hell.

"This isn't a conversation, is it? It's a threat."

"I only want you to see my imprisonment from my perspective," he said. "I was accused, tried, convicted, and sentenced in the blink of an eye."

Kendell had never been completely comfortable with Sanguine's actions. "I wasn't the one who cast you into hell. The malevolent spirit of Baron Samedi earned the harshest treatment among both the living and the dead, but you're only partly made up of his energy. However, as that part of you can't be removed, you have to suffer his fate."

"I'm first and foremost a businessman, and I know when I've gained all I'm likely to achieve in a negotiation. You understand my concerns about my judges and the consequence of the situation continuing as it stands, and I can see that my future depends on reconciling the two sides of my being. You and I are not at war any more than Baron Malveaux and Lincoln Laroque are in conflict within me. I simply must show you how my old lusts for power can be harnessed and directed. This has been a good meeting."

Kendell had the uneasy feeling she'd agreed to something without realizing it. "So now you'll help me get back to my life?"

"A deal is a deal."

∾

COLIN'S CONVERSATION with Kendell had been the longest talk he'd had with someone since entering hell. All that talking left his throat feeling like he'd just spent the night at a rave. Though he'd done most of his thinking out loud, the use of his voice for the benefit of another person left him light-headed. The discussion also exhausted most of his social skills. The combination of physical and emotional exercise left him content to walk the city streets in peace alongside the fetching young woman.

She stopped at the intersection of Royal and Canal. "I can understand lighting the streets, but why the streetcars?

They're lovely, but running them seems awfully frivolous for someone who prides himself on amassing power."

The casual conversation made him feel almost human. "Beyond the World Trade Center's built-in power containment, I haven't been able to find a way to store electricity. After a handful of lightning storms that emanated from the roof as the result of too much power, I thought it'd be best to siphon off the energy in a less dramatic fashion."

"Well, they're lovely."

He raised his hand as if hailing a cab. The red-and-yellow trolley clanked to a stop in front of them. "Your carriage awaits."

For a moment, he thought she was about to grace him with a feminine response of appreciation. Instead, she climbed aboard as if getting on a bus for her ride to work. "Agnes did a nice job of restoring this old streetcar. Don't you worry that by moving time forward, you'll lose the power of the hurricane?"

The familiar desire to dominate argued for him to sit as close to her as possible, invading her personal space and pinning her against the side of the streetcar. Instead, he took the bench across the aisle from her. "That building doesn't rely on only wind for power. You'd be amazed at what I've discovered. Luther not only put in solar power, but he also harnessed the flow of the Mississippi. Electricity isn't an issue, but storing up enough to move time is a challenge. That's where I need your help."

"I'm no mechanical engineer."

Her naivety made him smile. "I didn't expect you were.

What you do know, however, is how to harness the power of voodoo. Marie left some totems and, well, let's just say I drained their power."

"You mean when you broke into my ceremony to establish the seven gates."

She might be naïve, but she clearly wasn't stupid.

"I needed to get your attention. Had I not been so presumptuous as to butt into your game, you might not have returned."

She turned away from him. "Maybe it would be best if we didn't talk about how you've violated me with your display of power."

The way she phrased her response left him filled with both self-loathing and the familiar desire for conquest. "That was a long time ago."

"Not for me."

The streetcar rang its bell as it came to a stop at the end of Canal. They rode the elevator in silence up to the circular control room at the top of the structure.

Colin hadn't considered a woman's point of view for some time—even before being banished to hell—but as he looked around the room with someone at his side, he realized how haphazard the place looked. "Most of these controls run parts of the city, like the streetcars. The voodoo totems are spread around the room and roof. You'll find Marie's journals on the conference table."

She looked at him as though he'd forgotten something important. "And what am I supposed to do with them?"

"You're the expert at controlling evil spirits. Each totem contains multiple souls, though I'm sure you're familiar with how the fetishes work, having cast me into one of them. Having seen the hideous sculpture from the inside, I can tell you there's a power within the wood."

Her look almost resembled contrition. "The power works as a containment?"

"Not quite. The wooden figure feeds energy into the glass jar in its belly. The spirit remains conscious due to the nourishment. That's part of its torture. Since these are drained, the imprisoned spirits are dormant."

Her look changed from contrition to contempt. "And you want to repower these fetishes? What kind of sadistic devil are you? Why not let the spirits rest in peace?"

"I could ask you the same thing. Unlike me, however, my friends' punishments will serve the goal of getting you out of this time dimension. A lot of power can be stored in those ancient voodoo dolls."

She glanced through the first journal as though eyeing a used-book table at a charity fund-raiser. "You're counting on me doing evil to get away from you. This is your ultimate argument against me being some force for good, isn't it?"

"I'm not trying to trick you. These souls were imprisoned by Marie Laveau. She was the judge, jury, and jailor. We're simply using them like a landowner hiring a prison chain gang to clear his swamp."

She turned from the table and crossed her arms. "I still don't get it. You went to a lot of trouble to capture me for an afternoon chat. Now you're willing to use your secret stash of power to set me free. What's in it for you? And don't give me any bullshit about wanting to see the sun again. You could have done that by never zapping me in the first place. I'm also not buying that you just wanted to talk to me to present your case for clemency. You knew that was never going to happen. If I were to guess, I'd say you're about to imprison me in one of your little voodoo totems—probably as payback for my exorcism of you out of Myles."

"That's not a bad idea, but retaliation isn't a useful emotion in this empty hell—just a waste of energy. My preference would be for you to stay with me. I've been told that, given enough time, women find me quite charming."

"That's called Stockholm syndrome, not attraction."

"I'm constantly getting those two confused."

Her mouth remained tight, but her eyes told of the giggle that played inside her mind. "Jokes? Really?"

"A devil in his personal hell can't tell jokes?"

She turned back to the journals. "Not bad ones. You still haven't answered my question."

"I wanted to start a dialogue with you. If I keep you here any longer, you'll start complaining that you're my hostage. I've presented my case to the only person who would listen and was in a position to do something about it. Negotiations aren't always concluded in one sitting."

She set one of the journals next to a totem by the window—a good sign that he was making progress. "I don't expect our next meeting to be as dramatic."

He pulled off his cufflinks. "I'm sure you recognize these. Take one of them with you."

"I've cut my tie to the curse. And with you in hell, even Myles wouldn't be able to read you with one of the baron's possessions."

"You're a clever girl. You left that damn voodoo guitar pick here in hell. Now it contains the curse. That little guitar pick is a nine-volt battery compared to my nuclear reactor. However, that little hunk of voodoo-powered gold should be strong enough to power the connection between the two cufflinks."

She handled the piece of jewelry with her fingertips as if it were red hot. "And if I lock this thing up in some safe-deposit box? I'm not carrying it around with me."

"Must I figure everything out for you? In terms of voodoo technology, these cufflinks are like two tin cans and a string, and about as innocuous."

She nodded and stashed the piece of jewelry in her jeans pocket. "I still don't trust you."

"Life wouldn't be any fun if you did. Now, how do we power up these totems?"

---

6

*M*yles wasn't sure what to do. He'd been standing at the gate for five minutes. Kendell's trip, from his time perspective, should have been instantaneous. He needed to find Baron Samedi, but leaving the gate with the cane would close the door to the other realm. He looked down the hall. If someone saw him, there could end up being a rift between life and death.

A woman plowed into him so forcefully from the back that they both went tumbling to the floor.

"Thank God you're back," he said.

"Not so fast, bucko."

He rolled over and was shocked to see Sanguine but even more shocked that she had wings. "What in hell is going on?"

"Colin moved Kendell back in time. I needed to come tell you. Now I'm headed right back through the gate to get her."

The booming voice of Papa Ghede filled the hallway. "The hell you are."

Being caught by the head loa felt to Myles a little too much like seeing his father standing in the bedroom doorway while he had a girl on his bed. "I can explain."

"Baron Samedi filled me in. We need to get you out of the seventh gate before anyone else runs into you." Papa Ghede looked Sanguine over from head to toe. "Not very inconspicuous, are you?"

"A girl's gotta do what a girl's gotta do to survive in hell."

Papa Ghede didn't wait around for further small talk. "I've got a club next door. It's the kind of place where people don't ask questions. Follow me."

Myles felt like some notorious villain as he followed Papa Ghede out the back door and along the alleyway between the two buildings. At least Myles was dressed for the occasion. Sanguine, in her long white backless dress and wings, looked like a kid on her way to a school play. Her feathers rustled against every wall they passed.

When they were comfortably seated around a wooden bar table in the back room of Papa Ghede's establishment, Myles turned to Sanguine. "What happened?"

"Colin made it through Mary's first gate. We were headed over to confront him, but we were too late. He set loose a lightning storm from the World Trade Center. Next thing I knew, he and Kendell were gone."

Myles turned to Papa Ghede. "She's right. We have to go back. Right now."

The loa took a set of glass salt-and-pepper shakers and placed them next to each other. "It's not that simple. When you opened the gate, you shared a time frame. So long as you held the gate open, the time remained the same." He pulled the pepper shaker back toward him. "Then Kendell was sucked back in time. Bad, but not the worst situation. When Sanguine plowed through the gate, however, the door closed." He started moving the salt shaker forward one inch at a time. "Time is moving forward again for you. Even if Kendell was able to jump back to the starting point of when you first opened the door, we've moved past that point."

Myles thought his head was about to explode. "So she's trapped!"

"Not necessarily." Papa Ghede jumped the pepper shaker forward to where the salt was. "If she could figure out when you closed the door and how fast time is moving, she could calculate how far to jump forward. But as time isn't moving for her, you'd have to open the door at that moment."

"To the exact second? You're not leaving me much hope. And what if time isn't moving as fast here as she expects?"

Papa Ghede moved the pepper shaker the width of the salt container. "There's a time overlap, so she wouldn't need to hit it on the exact second—more like within a few minutes. That's why you needed to stand guard at the gate for more than just a second. As for our clocks, any realm that accepts embassies from other dimensions—the seven gates for example—agrees to use a uniform measure of time. It wouldn't do for someone to walk into the bank in their thirties and come out an hour later in their seventies. And before you get any bright ideas about rushing into her dimension, remember: someone needs to hold the door open."

Myles put the cane on the table. "Can't you do it?"

"Not my job. We gave you that staff for a reason. The gate between hell and Guinee is sealed shut. You're breaking into Colin's realm. We can't be a part of your misconduct."

Sanguine took the salt shaker and scattered the granules across the table. "I'm not burdened with a body. Kendell and I are linked, and with the lifeline Myles established, I can pull myself back to him. I'll go find her and bring her back. It's really the only answer."

Myles couldn't believe he agreed with Sanguine. "Just be quick. The band was fading fast when Kendell and I came looking for you. If you exhaust their spiritual energy, you may lose your way home, not to mention the effect your actions will have on those women."

～

Sanguine didn't consider Myles stupid, just easily manipulated. She liked that in a guy. The dudes who were constantly questioning her motivations or loyalties were just looking for a fight. Not that she minded a good confrontation from time to time, but when there was work to be done, she much preferred a guy who would appreciate her brilliance.

She stopped him before he reopened the broom closet. "I don't know how long this will take. Even with Papa Ghede's explanation, I might be gone more than five minutes. But I promise that when I return, I'll have Kendell with me."

"Don't go doing something stupid like pursuing Colin. Just find Kendell, and get your asses back here."

Even easily manipulated dudes had backbones sometimes, especially if they weren't dumb and were worried about their girlfriends.

"I can't be expected to answer for my actions if I run into him," she said.

"Likewise. I'm just saying *this* time, save Kendell. Colin can wait for another day."

"Any ideas on how to zoom in on her time zone?" She didn't like accepting restrictions, but once Kendell was out of hell, Sanguine would once again be free to do as she pleased. Plus, Colin had made it clear that time travel was possible for him. All she had to do was sneak into the World Trade Center and find out what he'd been up to.

He opened the door and put the cane across the top of the doorway. "You were the one who said it would be like scattering salt on the table."

She shrugged. "I needed something to tell that loa of yours. The last thing I need is interference from some voodoo lord."

From the way Myles crinkled up his face, she suspected he wanted to argue the merits of telling the loas the truth. Fortunately for him, he refrained. "If Cheesecake were here, she'd know how to bark such that Kendell would hear her across time, but I'm afraid you're on your own."

Sanguine wasn't typically a fan of displays of emotion, especially to guys who she wasn't sleeping with, but she couldn't help leaning in and kissing him on the cheek. "You're quite brilliant when you're not trying to be." Without waiting for him to demand an explanation, she rushed through the open door to hell.

She ran out of the bank and straight into the swarm of dragonflies she'd summoned. "You guys have the biggest bug eyes I can imagine. So if any insect can see far enough into the past, it would be you. Go find my friend."

As the long-winged insects flew away, their number was reduced by half. She mentally bonded with the nearest dragonfly before it had time to fly out of sight. Instead of focusing on the present or future, its attention was fixed on the past. It was flying forward, but everything around it was moving backward. It continued on its trajectory, and the future view became the past since that was where it was headed. *So that's how you do it.*

Though she had work to do and a promise to keep, Sanguine couldn't help trying out the lesson the dragonflies had revealed. She jumped off the top step of the bank and spread her wings. Trying to focus on the past, which was like a film running backward through a projector, was confusing enough from the bug's perspective. As an angel prone to crash landings, Sanguine headed above the buildings for self-preservation.

She caught sight of the dragonfly who'd originally shown her the time-defying maneuver. As the only object moving forward, he wasn't hard to miss. Other dragonflies passed him flying both forward and backward. As they did, she became diverted by their consciousness. The phenomenon became clear when she spotted another angel in white whizzing past her. *So that's why so many of you insects look exactly alike. You're all the same being, just at different points in your time travel. I guess I'd better pay attention to where and when I'm flying to avoid plowing into myself.*

Darkness fell, and her insect companion drifted off to find a quiet place to wait out the night. When the rain began pelting her wings from below, she realized he was the smart one.

She settled back to the steps of the bank. As if someone had shifted the rain from reverse to forward, the drops once again fell from the sky. In her multitime vision, she could again see the future as the future and not farther into the past. *Time travel must only work when I'm flying. Strange.* The rain began a rhythmic tapping so monotonously regular that she knew she'd slipped into Colin's no-time version of hell. She could still see what was coming at her, but when it came to her grandmother's version of the natural elements, things were once again at a standstill.

She tried to work out how traveling into the past, seeing another version of herself, and the lack of time dimension interacted. *There should only be one of me here and now. I could go forward in time and come back later, meaning there would be two of me, but I think I would know. I could feel those multiple dragonflies as one being, just as I would have known without seeing that the second angel was also me. So I've only made this trip back to this exact moment once.*

The effort made her head hurt. "Fuck this. I'm a swamp witch, not a theoretical physicist."

She didn't even know if Colin was in this time zone. The lust to hunt him down and continue her plan conflicted with her promise to keep her mission focused on saving Kendell. "I'm letting you off the hook this time, devil. I've learned what I needed to know about time. Our paths will cross again."

She leapt back into the air. A dozen dragonflies met her —each its own being—and guided her into the future.

Kendell sat on the top step of the bank, wondering what the hell she was supposed to do. She'd made it back to the time frame she'd left, but the gate back to Guinee had closed. She had no way of knowing how long Myles had kept his vigil. She could only imagine the torment he had to be going through.

Without a way back to Guinee, she was stumped. Her first thought was to wander down to the Scratchy Dog and hope her band members were keeping an eye out for her through their gate. But as the gate was geared for Colin, and she'd left him in the past, the idea seemed hopeless. Approaching all seven gates in order was an option. After all, that was their reason for existence—to let someone from hell back into life. Baron Samedi, however, had proven that a guardian stuck on the wrong side of his gate couldn't be the one to open it. Unlike him, she didn't have a Papa Ghede to fill the void. Opening the other six gates, without being able to open hers as well, might too easily make Colin's escape inevitable.

A dragonfly buzzed its wings in front of her like pages of a book being riffled by the wind. "Hello, little guy."

Another joined the first, and then another, until a dozen dragonflies were eyeing her as if they found her an oddity in their insect world.

"I'm working on a way out. If any of you have any suggestions, I'm all ears."

Kendell didn't really expect an answer, but as they all turned and flew off, she wondered if they knew something she didn't.

They came back like a fighter squadron that had split off in all directions. A second later, Sanguine materialized out of thin air and plowed into her.

Kendell helped the disoriented angel to her feet. "Those bugs friends of yours?"

"Just my grains of salt."

Kendell said, "Come again?"

"Inside joke."

"We're the only two people in this dimension. You can't get more inside than that."

Sanguine shook the rain out of her wings and spread them so the sun shone through the translucent feathers. "I'm sure Myles could explain it far better than I can. Now, let's get you back to his time zone so we can blow this hellhole."

"You know how?" Kendell asked. "What are we waiting for?"

"I'll have to take you for a little flight. My dragonfly buddies will show the way. You might find the trip a little disorienting. I know I do."

Kendell turned around so Sanguine could wrap her arms around her waist. "Great. I'm trusting my life to an angel who gets confused in flight and smacks into walls."

"Be nice. I'm no angel."

Kendell crossed her arms over her chest. "Why are we flying when the front door to the bank is right there?"

Sanguine held her tightly and jumped into the air. "I can only move through time while I'm in the air. There are limitations to what I can do."

The insects moved in a dizzying array as they led the way into the future, but Kendell could only see what was happening right in front of her. "What are you seeing?"

"I get a multioptical vision of the past, present, and future, but I can only see a few moments at a time. Now, hush up, or I'll miss my landing spot."

Kendell closed her eyes, fearful she was going to be Sanguine's airbag on impact. To her relief, she felt the ground gently come up under her feet. "Nice landing."

"I'm working on it. Now, let's get you through that gate before Myles pulls off my feathers."

Kendell feared she was in for a fight. "You are coming with me."

"Are you crazy? Now that I can fly, see the future, and travel in time, I can go after Colin. I only promised to return you to Myles."

Kendell suspected arguing with her guardian angel wasn't the best idea. "I don't give a shit what you told Myles. Do you have any idea how much we spent on that couch? I'd like it back, Sleeping Beauty."

"I'm not arguing this with you again. I've got a mission to accomplish."

If arguing with an angel was a bad idea, Kendell thought punching her would definitely be frowned upon. She struggled to keep her cool. "You know that's not what I meant. I need you back among the living. No one understands me the way you do. We're two halves of this puzzle, and I don't like you rushing off to fight the devil alone."

"I'll walk with you to the door to Guinee to make sure Myles is still there, but I'm not crossing over with you. Now, where did you leave that little turd of a devil?"

Kendell considered not telling Sanguine, but she feared that would only make her more determined. "I left him in the past."

Sanguine frowned in apparent confusion. "How did you manage that?"

"He's figured out how to move time forward and backward as if he were turning an old-fashioned movie reel by hand in a projector. What I figured out from Marie's journals was how to step from one frame to the corresponding frame in the next coil on the spool."

"Doesn't sound very precise."

"I had to do something," Kendell said. "Any time was better than sharing that moment with Colin."

Sanguine led the way up the steps. "So long as he's trapped in the past, I'll find him."

Kendell followed her, hoping Myles had a more convincing argument to make Sanguine return home. When they got to the large office, she was surprised to see Papa Ghede standing next to Myles in the interdimensional doorway.

"Thank God and the loas of the dead!" Myles gave her a look of relief that filled her with love.

Papa Ghede stood aside from the door. "We'd better get

moving. The sooner we get the three of you out of Guinee, the better for everyone, alive and dead."

Sanguine stood at the entrance of the office. "You're getting a little ahead of yourself, old man. I'm not leaving hell."

Kendell wondered how anyone survived the original loa's glare of displeasure. "You have to go. Leaving your body uninhabited by a soul is a sure way of turning it into a zombie. A living soul wandering around Guinee with five-foot-long wings doesn't exactly go unnoticed. Someone's going to get the bright idea that there's a body among the living for the taking. I can only hold back the tide for so long. Stay in hell, and the loas of the dead will invade your grandmother's creation and drag you out by your feathers."

Kendell hadn't processed all the dangers of taking Sanguine's body out of hell while comatose, but then, she hadn't yet realized the young woman had gone for a little spiritual joy ride either. "I'm no longer asking," she said. "I'm telling. Get through that fucking door. We'll discuss what to do about Colin over coffee and beignets. I don't care if you do have wings. I can still kick your butt, and you know it. This isn't just about you anyway. My bandmates are withering away while you're on this vendetta. Move it, sister."

For the first time that Kendell could remember, Sanguine backed down instead of rising to the fight. "I love you too." Meekly, she walked ahead of Kendell and through the gate that Myles held open.

7

*S*anguine sat on the couch in Kendell and Myles's apartment, feeling like an angel who'd had her wings clipped. Having Delphine de Galpion poke and prod her while filling the room with noxious scents from her voodoo candles didn't help at all.

"I'm fine. Why can't you all just leave me alone for once?"

Madam de Galpion's eyes looked like they were floating in the haze. "I'm not checking for any ill side effects. Though spending a month in hell wasn't the smartest move. Your body wasn't meant to be left unattended for that long."

Kendell hovered around like an overly protective mother hen. "Baron Samedi said she might suffer from some permanent version of déjà vu. He called it *déjà vecu*. Can you tell how far off she is in her perception of time?"

The whole experience was giving Sanguine a splitting

headache. "Far enough ahead that I've been able to block out this conversation."

The dark woman motioned for Myles to open the French doors. The fresh air was probably meant to help Sanguine's disposition. It didn't work.

Madam de Galpion snuffed out her odious candles. "With Sanguine bouncing around in hell's perverted concept of time, it's impossible to know how far off she is. My guess is she can see days—maybe a week—into the future clearly. She'll probably get hazy images as far as a month in advance. But time isn't always a smooth-running river. What she sees won't necessarily happen. The more intense the event, the more likely it will happen. But ask her if it's safe to eat the rest of that muffuletta that Myles put in the fridge a week ago, and her accuracy will be anyone's guess."

Sanguine leaned forward conspiratorially toward Kendell. "The answer will always be no."

She could feel the puppy's eyes on her long before the little ball of black fur jumped onto the couch. He sat at attention and stared at her as if he too were a voodoo practitioner trying to read her aura. His single bark echoed three times in her head.

"Hey, knock that off." Something about the dog felt all too familiar. "You're from my grandmother's hell."

Myles at least understood the connection. "You can experience his past, present, and future, can't you?"

"Only for a moment. Those bug eyes I wore in hell must have left me with some awareness when it comes to hell's creatures."

Myles sat next to the dog and scratched his head. "Doughnut Hole may be from hell, but he's not bound to it. And he's not a creature. He's a dog."

"I didn't mean any disrespect. I'm not always the most diplomatic while I'm processing new information. If it wasn't for him, his sisters, and their mother, we'd all be in deep trouble. But if I can see his past and future, I should be able to see Colin's too—should he end up in this reality. I'm not sure that does us any good, but it's interesting."

Madam de Galpion was still loading her magic tricks into her bag. "You're still afraid he'll find a way out of your hell?"

Sanguine found it hard not to take offense at the voodoo jab against the presumed weaknesses of her grandmother's Wiccan invention. "He's not a devil of our creation. Though the difference between our religions works to hold him captive, it's not like I can anticipate his every move. Just once, I'd like to see you take some responsibility for you and your ancestor's actions." Sanguine hadn't meant to be so confrontational, but the voodoo priestess had gotten on her last nerve with those damn scents.

"I was simply trying to figure out if I needed to keep my voodoo cabinets locked tight. From Kendell's description of events, it sounds like he took a liking to my spirit totems."

"Sorry. Getting used to this body again has taken a toll on my emotions. I feel like I'm getting a double whammy of PMS."

Kendell waved some of the voodoo smoke out the window. "Sounds like a good time for me to take you out for those beignets I promised."

Sanguine could already taste the sweet goodness. "Yes, please."

Getting out of the apartment helped lift her mood, as did being alone with Kendell. The streets were filled with people. The strangers were like moving partitions that Sanguine tried to avoid. She walked on the balls of her feet, imagining she could once again hop into the air and spread her wings. Instead, she plowed into an overweight tourist in gaudy shorts and a Hawaiian shirt.

"Watch where you're going!" the man said.

I'll bet you'd sing a different tune if you could see me as hell's angel. People bugged her to begin with. Taking offense after spending so much time in an almost deserted dimension wasn't going to help her disposition.

"I miss my wings," she whispered to Kendell.

"After breakfast, we'll work on that vision issue. Knowing what's coming at you might help."

They didn't resume their conversation until they were seated at a quiet table in a small courtyard with their coffees and beignets.

Sanguine knew she had a lot to apologize for. "I must have freaked you out when you couldn't wake me up."

"Charlie offered to wake you with a kiss, but I declined on your behalf."

Though Myles's fellow bartender wasn't the worst of his friends, he was too much of a lothario to even be considered as boyfriend material, let alone Prince Charming. "I appreciate that. You didn't consider trying to kiss me yourself?"

Kendell snickered. "I have a boyfriend."

Sanguine took the levity as a good starting point to getting serious with her emotions. "I wanted to apologize, and say thank you, but I'm not good at either."

Kendell held her hand. "You don't have to."

"You were right about me having to come back to my body, but don't get any ideas that I'm going to listen in the future. That was a one-time admission."

"Apology accepted, or was that a thank-you?"

Sanguine grimaced at the cut. "I'm not sure. I told you I sucked at this stuff."

Kendell leaned back in the chair with her coffee. "Then let's talk about what you are good at. Without returning to hell, what do you propose we do about Colin?"

"You're sticking with your refusal to let me kill him?"

"You've just come from Guinee. Do you honestly believe those loas stand a chance against him?"

"Good point," Sanguine said. "I fear we're back where we started."

"Not quite. He has made it through the first gate, but now we know he's just being his manipulative self again."

Sanguine peered over her cup at Kendell. "What did he want with you anyway?"

"To plead his case."

"Just like a guy—doesn't know how to take rejection."

Kendell's blush told Sanguine all she really needed to know.

"He might have a slight crush on me," Kendell said, "but our conversation was civil. For a devil infected with a misogynistic asshole, Colin can still pull out the charm."

"Listen, sister, we're going to destroy him. Maybe I can't

kill him, but that hell is too good for him. Don't go getting soft on me. You said it yourself—you already have a boyfriend." Sanguine had never been prouder of herself for not slapping some sense into Kendell.

"I just told you so you would know I see what he's doing. I'm not naïve. In fact, I bet I'm more experienced with guys than you. His charm doesn't work on me, but his infatuation is something we can use."

Though Kendell was probably right, Sanguine could see that using her as bait would only call Colin forth. "How is it that guys, and girls for that matter, willingly follow you into hell? Maybe we should just make a Kendell voodoo-sex doll and leave it in his office. We'd never hear from him again."

"Be nice. It's not as if going after him like some avenging angel with creepy insect eyes worked all that well at keeping him in his dimension."

"My intention," Sanguine said, "wasn't to make him happy with his situation. My aim was to kill him and remove all traces of his existence. A plan, by the way, which I still think could work if only it didn't violate your two restrictions of not returning to hell and not killing him."

Kendell put the cup back on the table in favor of the powdered-sugar-covered beignet. "I'm sticking by my requirements. He'd only end up—"

Sanguine raised her hand. "I know. You don't have to make your case again. My plan does require a certain degree of competence among the loas of the dead while I complete my mission. So back to what we now know that we didn't before. He has a crush on you."

"And you can sprout wings and see into the future and past."

Sanguine stuck her tongue at Kendell. "He can't be trusted, but we did already know that. I guess even with age, he's not changing."

Kendell squirmed in her chair. "In exchange for having our conversation, he helped me get back to my time. Unfortunately, Myles had already left."

"No need to thank me."

She shook her head as though an idea was having trouble forming. "I do appreciate your rescue, but that's not my point. You said he can't be trusted. Everything he does is with some ulterior motive."

Sanguine felt a cold chill run down her spine. "What did he have you do?"

"He said there wasn't enough energy to send me forward through time." She looked up. "We need to go to the World Trade Center. I have to talk to Luther Noire. That's where Colin is getting his electricity, and I just gave him a fucking power converter."

KENDELL THREW some money on the table and got up without waiting for the check. Sanguine rushed after her. "So what's your plan? We just walk into Luther's office and have a nice chat over tea while he bullshits us again about doing something? You know, you're like the hero version of the villain who sets up a slow death for her adversary then walks away assuming everything will go according to plan. You have too much faith in people."

Though Kendell didn't like being made fun of, she knew Sanguine had a point. "Nice to see you're back to your usual self. To answer your question, no. I have no plan to listen to more of his justifications and avoidance. We're going to burn that building to the ground, paranormally speaking."

Sanguine pointed down a side street. "Aren't we going to need some voodoo bombs or something? Scratch and Sniff is that way."

"I'm also done being manipulated by Delphine. We don't need anything she has anyway."

"Nice to see you're coming around to my way of thinking, but shouldn't we at least snag Myles? He's proven useful in a pinch before."

"He wouldn't agree to what I have in mind." Once Kendell had something in mind, she was like a hurricane— only small deviations were accepted.

Sanguine had to hurry to keep up. "Is this what it's like to be you when I get hardheaded?"

"Probably."

Finally, she grabbed Kendell's arm. "Stop. We have to talk about this. You can't just go storming into that tower expecting to pull it down through force of will."

"Watch me."

Sanguine stopped walking and clinched onto Kendell's wrist like an anchor. "Kendell, you at least owe me an explanation of what we're walking into. You might not always agree with my plans, but I do share them with you before marching into battle."

"I didn't ask you to join me."

Sanguine spun her around with such force Kendell nearly lost her footing. "You're being obstinate for no reason. Talk to me."

Kendell had no interest in venting her anger before it was needed, but she did owe her cohort at least a reason for the attack. "Colin tricked me into loading up Marie's voodoo totems with energy. Now he knows how to turn that electricity gathered by the World Trade Center into a source of voodoo magic. And we know he already used those dolls as his creepy-clown way of infiltrating our seven-gates house of mirrors. Put it all together, and I just gave him the keys for walking out of hell. I have to stop him. We don't need anything or anybody because everything's already up on the top floor of that fucking building. I just need to get up there."

"And you think Luther's just going to let you in?"

They were wasting time. "Nope. Either Colin is paying Luther—manipulating him like he does everyone else—or he has simply stolen the building. Whatever the situation, going through Luther will only alert Colin to what I'm doing. Satisfied?"

"Satisfied. Any ideas on how to get into the structure? The few times I was there, it felt like a paranormal Fort Knox." Sanguine let go of Kendell's wrist.

Kendell resumed her march toward the river. "The front door is guarded, but the basement entrance from Harrah's underground parking lot isn't. I need to access those turbines first anyway."

"That whole place is guarded, under video surveillance,

and probably booby-trapped. I'm not trying to stop you, just point out the obvious."

For the first time since the guilt had taken control of Kendell's thoughts, she stopped her advance. "You're right, but there is someone who can get us in." She pointed to the grand police station.

Sanguine's look of shock nearly made Kendell laugh. "You can't be serious. Lieutenant Cazenave? We *know* he was working for Luther."

"Joe works for a number of organizations," Kendell said, "but he's only loyal to doing what's right. He's gone up against his own police force to help us. I trust him, maybe even more than I do myself."

Sanguine nodded. "You are a pretty shady character. Have you given any thought to the fact that you might be arrested just for setting foot inside the station?"

Kendell tried to run down all the events that had happened since her first excursion into the paranormal world. "They don't have anything on either of us. Myles did steal Luther's van, but I doubt they'd press charges."

"You seem to be forgetting one pretty big problem: Colin Malveaux is missing. The most powerful businessman in New Orleans, not to mention the nephew of the chief of police, isn't someone to slip under the radar. And sister, are one of the most logical suspects."

"You might have a point there. Chief Laroque did meet with Myles, though, to explain the dangers when Lincoln became Colin."

Sanguine wrapped her arms around her stomach. "Yeah, but in private, in the dead of night, and in a place where he was certain the cameras and the other observation devices had been shut off. I don't think you're going to be able to count on his help. Do you have any other way of contacting Lieutenant Cazenave without walking directly into a prison cell?"

Even sending Myles wouldn't do much good. Whatever beef the cops had with him that had resulted in his apartment being under surveillance had never been explained. Kendell's only real hope regarding the police was the fact that Joe had worn his police uniform during the team's second line out of hell. That simple indicator that he was back on the force had meant she and Myles no longer had to watch their backs, but Sanguine was right. If she did something stupid like unintentionally turning herself in, Joe was not likely to fix it.

"I'm open to any ideas."

Sanguine nodded as if accepting the position. "I can do it. They don't know me in there. Joe Cazenave has seen me with you, so it's not like we won't recognize each other, but the rest of the force would just discount me as some girl from the bayou lost in the big city."

Kendell would have played an entire gig for free for a better idea. "Be careful. Don't say anything incriminating inside that building. You have to assume you're being listened to at all times. I just need Joe to come out, so I can explain the situation."

Sanguine quickly reverted from helper to snarky critic. "I am familiar with eavesdropping. I am a witch, you know."

Kendell headed to the coffee shop across from the police station while Sanguine walked through the wrought-iron gate and past the line of parked police scooters. Kendell didn't need the caffeine, but after years of being a barista, she'd been conditioned to find comfort in the hot beverage. She sat at a table close to the window and tried not to stare at the station's front door. Her leg twitched uncontrollably. Putting her free hand on her knee only moved the nervous movement to her fingers, which were wrapped around the coffee cup on the table. *This is insane. How the hell did Myles stand at that gate, waiting for me, without losing his mind?*

The thought of him at home with the two dogs calmed her down. In spite of what she'd told Sanguine, she did want Myles with her. He had a way of seeing things with a clarity that often defied emotion. He was bound to be furious at finding out she'd acted without consulting him. For a moment, she considered running the couple of blocks to their apartment while Sanguine made her case to whatever cop she'd run into. Really, it all came down to the dogs. If Kendell did end up behind bars, Cheesecake and Doughnut Hole deserved to have Myles looking out for them.

She had downed half her cup of coffee when she caught sight of Sanguine's long hair in her peripheral vision. Joe was beside her at the counter, ordering drinks. *You fucking could have let me know you were safe.* Her emotional response was quickly quashed by the understanding of the need to remain inconspicuous.

They came to her table as if Joe was just on a coffee break. He set his cup down. "I won't ask if you've lost your mind. Clearly, you're suffering from some form of amnesia if you think you can just break into Luther's offices."

Kendell glared at Sanguine. "I only wanted you to get

him. I told you not to say anything that would give us away in that building."

Sanguine shrugged off the attack. "He assured me his office was safe. My feminine charms only go so far."

"Maybe if you had just said it was for me and not tried to flirt with him, you wouldn't have had to explain our need for him."

Joe put his hand on the table as if setting up a barrier between contestants. "Stop bickering if you want to remain undetected. In case you hadn't noticed, cops and coffee have a way of going together. This establishment's location isn't by chance."

Kendell closed her eyes at her stupidity. "Where can we talk in private?"

He picked up his cup. "It's a nice day. Let's head out to the river."

The casual nature of the encounter contrasted drastically with Kendell's desire to bust down the doors of the World Trade Center, but she kept her cool, knowing that acting like Sanguine wasn't going to help their situation. Joe's meandering path through the Quarter to the river wasn't helping with her anxiety one bit, but she assumed he was making sure they weren't being followed. By the time they'd found a metal bench where they could conduct their conversation, she felt like she was about to leave her body and fly at the building the way Sanguine had done as the avenging angel.

"Okay, we're here," she said. "What do you want to know?"

Joe had a look of deliberate calm in the face of danger

that spoke volumes about his military training. "What has you so worked up, other than Colin figuring out how to convert energy? No matter what time zone he's in, there wouldn't be enough wind force to generate the power needed. If you can convince me of the danger, I promise you, I can make Luther listen. His allegiance is to protect the living from the beyond."

Kendell hadn't bothered analyzing the underlying problem, but Joe's calm helped her focus. "I don't believe Luther's in control any longer. From the moment Colin used the power of that building to infect our creation of the seven gates, I assumed he'd usurped Luther as the one in charge. Honestly, I doubt Luther could even open the doors at this point."

Joe listened intently. "And if he has taken control?"

"Item one was gaining command of Luther's isolation chambers for those paranormal artifacts. From the way Luther described the building, it harnesses the wind to run the chambers like cooling ponds keeping plutonium rods from overheating in a nuclear reactor. But Colin flipped the switch. Instead of keeping all the magical objects in stasis, he's used them to power up that building. He no longer needs the wind. He's got all the energy he'll ever need. That's what he was unintentionally showing me. In his arrogance, he had the whole city running like a child's toy train set with lit-up buildings and everything. I should have seen what he was up to."

Sanguine put her hand over Kendell's. "You couldn't have known what he really had going on. He's an expert at manipulation."

The comfort from the young witch who was always busting Kendell's ovaries didn't help at all. "When you start offering me sympathy, I know I've really fucked up."

"I didn't mean it like that. So what do we do?"

Kendell turned back to Joe. "The basement is full of turbines and other machinery that must be used to keep the magical objects in check. From what I saw in Colin's hell, he's got all of the controls upstairs in the old circular restaurant. Since he's not in this dimension, we can't use his controls."

Joe stared at the top of the building. "That's why you think Luther can't even open a door, isn't it? If he could, he would have taken back control. He's not the type to accept incarceration without a fight."

Even with his air of military reserve, Kendell could tell Joe was concerned for Luther's safety, and with good reason. "Colin wouldn't destroy an asset. My guess is Luther is locked in his office. The man still has more knowledge of that building than anyone alive. Colin is more interested in containing an adversary than destroying him."

Joe looked down and nodded. "Luther can take care of himself, but losing control isn't an insult he'll take lightly. As for the basement equipment, it maintains a dimensional shift around the objects—basically the cooling water in your nuclear analogy. On their own, the objects wouldn't pose a threat even if they were left out in the open, but if that soothing dimension were turned into an irritating hell, they would all get spun up."

"So he hasn't just turned off the equipment?" Sanguine asked.

Joe shook his head. "If that had been the case, the objects would show up in our reality."

Fuck. Fuck. Fuck. Kendell had played right into Colin's hands. "He needed to combat the cooling effects from our turbines while not losing the objects to our dimension. In cases of city power outages, electricity provided by the wind from the storm is gathered by the building. Marie Laveau's totems also use naturally occurring energy to contain her prisoners in their spirit jars. All Colin had to do was direct that hell-dimension wind energy through the totems to irritate the paranormal objects into providing enough power to run his little make-believe version of New Orleans. He's smart enough to notice that his creation would only be running at partial power. The turbines would be trying to calm the objects while his voodoo dolls would be working as irritants. The real trick was routing the energy from the basement turbines through the voodoo totems and then back down into the paranormal-object vaults. By modifying Marie's totems into accepting all available power—not just that which was naturally occurring—I inadvertently gave him the answer."

Sanguine got up and started pacing the way Myles did when he was working out a solution. *"Now* can I kill him?"

"I was only trying to lay out the blueprint of the problem. Shutting off the turbines won't help at this point. Now that he's revved up the objects beyond critical mass, cooling them down again won't be so simple. His paranormal-energy generation is self-sustaining."

Joe pointed toward the river beyond the building. "There is a failsafe. Just like nuclear reactors, the World Trade

Center was built next to the water for a reason. The vaults can be jettisoned into the river."

Kendell couldn't even imagine the effect of so many magical objects released back into the public's hands. "That sounds a mite extreme."

"Last resorts tend to be that way," Joe said. "And the only way is to access the vaults remotely. The thinking was that if the objects became unstable, the World Trade Center itself would be unsafe. So they kept the controls for the ejections separate from the building."

Kendell hoped for a better answer but accepted that she had to be prepared for the worst. "Where?"

"Saint Louis Cathedral. Luther wanted the controls in a building that wasn't likely to be demolished. The Catholic Church is pretty good at keeping up its sanctuaries. The bishop is the only one who knows how to access the controls. I'm not recommending the failsafe, mind you. I just thought you should know it exists."

Kendell looked past Jackson Square at the cathedral that dominated the skyline. Sending someone there as backup made sense, but she needed both Joe and Sanguine if they were to enter the World Trade Center. "There's simply too much to do for just the three of us. I'm sorry, Sanguine, you were right. The only way I know how to change a dimension is with music, and for a building that big, I'm going to need the band. We'll also need Myles and his cane so we can move between dimensions."

Joe got up and turned away from the World Trade Center. "I'll get Professor Yates. He's pretty smart when it comes to paranormal machinery."

Sanguine looked from the French Quarter to the Marigny. "Do you want me to fetch Myles?"

"Round up the band," Kendell said. "While you're at it, you might think about thanking them for the energy they pumped into you—or apologize for sucking them dry like a vampire. I'll get Myles."

"What about Delphine?" Joe asked. "Those totems did come from her shop."

Kendell had to admit that she had changed her views about Delphine. As always, she was slow to convince, especially when Myles was doing the arguing, but once on board, she was fully committed. "Myles was right. I no longer trust her—not that she made any secret of her allegiances. Those are her ancestor's totems up there, and when this is over, I suspect Luther is going to demand they be turned over to him and his vaults. We can't risk her hidden agenda."

---

8

*M*yles was beginning to feel a little like a glorified dog sitter and interdimensional doorman. Not that he had any specific skills when it came to keeping Colin in his hell, but being relegated to holding the door open hurt his pride. He did have to admit, though, that minding the Scratchy Dog and tending bar with Charlie weren't bad ways of spending his nights. And Doughnut Hole loved having his human companion available at any time of the day. As for Cheesecake, she accepted Myles as a poor substitute for her mistress, but he didn't take it personally.

The light of late afternoon streamed in from the French doors and illuminated Kendell as she stood panting in the doorway of their apartment. Her look of panic had become all too familiar. "I need your help."

"Don't tell me—Colin did something dangerous, and it's

up to you to save the world. Do I get to do more than just hold the door for you this time?"

"I don't have time to explain. When this is over, I promise I'll make it up to you, but right now, I really need you to just come with me."

Kendell really wasn't good at apologies.

"I just want to make one thing clear first—I'm not sitting on the sidelines again while you rush headfirst into danger. We're supposed to be partners."

She lowered her arms and sighed. "We are partners. I know lately I've sucked at being a girlfriend. I promise I'm not taking you for granted. And you're right. Colin has done something stupid, and I do have to save humanity again. But this time it's my fault. Now, will you please get off your ass, so you can save mine?"

He couldn't hold his anger for long. "It is an awfully cute ass."

"Bring your cane. We have some interdimensional issues."

He snagged the walking stick from behind the door. "We are going to talk later. This discussion isn't over."

She batted her eyes at him. "Yes, sir."

He knew he was being played, but he also knew she'd never act the submissive girl with anyone but him. He patted her playfully on the butt as she led the way out of the apartment. "I love you, but I'm serious."

"I know."

He gave the dogs one last look before locking the door. "So what's the mythical adventure this time?"

"I fucked up."

She wasn't usually one for self-condemnation. Her guilty plea drove aside his irritation at being taken for granted. "What's going on? The more I know about what we're walking into, the better prepared I'll be to help you."

"In getting back to you at the gate to Guinee—which I never thanked you for or acknowledged how dangerous that must have been for you—I think I showed Colin how to use the energy from the World Trade Center to punch a hole from hell to life."

He gripped his cane, ready for action. "Okay, that's bad. I assume the others are meeting up with us?"

"Sanguine's getting the band, and Joe is on the hunt for Professor Yates."

He couldn't help noticing the obvious omission. "Should I even ask?"

She took his hand and held it close to her side as they hurried out of their apartment building and into the busy streets of the French Quarter. "You were right about Delphine too. I don't trust her. I can't promise to listen every time you give me advice, but I will try to do better in the future."

He lifted her hand and kissed it. "I love that you're headstrong and able to save the world all by yourself. Just know that you don't have to. Now, what's your plan for Colin?"

"First we have to shut down his ability to leave hell. Everything depends on Delphine's old voodoo totems."

He scratched his head with the silver skull handle of the cane. "I still don't get how he could handle her voodoo dolls when the one he'd been trapped in wasn't in his dimension."

"I wondered about that. The best answer I could come up with was that Delphine's shop is one of those embassies Baron Samedi talked about. Because she housed all Marie's voodoo collection, the shop acted as the same interdimensional bridge as the World Trade Center. You know how objects under Luther's care can exist independent of dimension? These places are like neutral zones. The totem Colin was locked in was in his office when he was cast into hell, so it wasn't protected, interdimensionally speaking. When Agnes Delarosa powered up her realm, the totem—being voodoo in origin—didn't make the transition."

He wondered if he'd ever be able to keep all the puzzle pieces straight. "So we need to bring those totems he stole from Delphine's shop in his hell dimension back from his realm into ours—preferably without involving Delphine."

She stopped walking so abruptly he had to look back to find her. "This is why not including you from the beginning was such a phenomenal mistake on my part. I was trying to figure out how to power down the totems, but stealing them back cuts off his ability to direct the energy he's building up. He can have all the bullets he wants, but it won't do him any good if he doesn't have a gun to fire them."

Though her praise warmed his heart, he wasn't about to discount Colin's ability to wriggle out of a noose. "I'm positive he'll look for another way to use that power, but at least it'll stop him for the moment."

"And if he sees that we can take his toys from him, he might even think twice about trying to abduct one of us again."

Myles had never been comfortable with the interest Colin had shown in Kendell, no matter what persona he chose. "I know it's a little early to be demanding concessions from you, but if it's all the same, I'd rather you didn't try to face him alone again."

"I didn't intend to make it a personal conversation last time. I was with Sanguine. Colin abducted me with his lightning-bolt time-bending machine."

"I wasn't just talking about this latest tête-a-tête. He seems to find ways of getting you alone. I trust you, but I think we can both agree his intentions are never honorable. I'm worried for your safety."

"This isn't the time. I can take care of myself, but I'll take your request under advisement."

He figured he'd pushed as hard as he dared. He looked up at the empty building at the foot of Canal Street. "You know, I really wish someone would redevelop that thing."

Her snicker told him he'd been forgiven for being the overly protective, jealous boyfriend. "Sure would make our lives easier. Maybe Luther could move his operation into a mountain cave in Tibet. Anywhere but New Orleans."

"I hear Atlantis in nice."

Joe jogged up to them carrying his customary paramilitary gear in a backpack covered with touristy French Quarter stickers. Even in his city camouflage, Joe's muscular physique and determined movements made it hard to see him as anything other than a commando looking for action.

Kendell looked around. "Where's the professor?"

"I dropped him off at the cathedral. As he's the most

technologically savvy, I thought he'd be best at helping with the failsafe if we run into trouble."

Though Myles had said he wanted to be filled in, taking time to learn the details of whatever backup plan might be in place didn't sound productive to their quest. "Can you still get us into the basement?"

"I can," Joe said, "but if Luther is locked in his office, I doubt the elevators will be running. It's a long climb up thirty-four floors."

Kendell felt her biceps. "Especially if we have to lug all our music equipment up to the top. Once we're up there, I can focus the band's energy, but I can't force the sound to cross dimensions."

Myles lifted his cane. "That's why you brought me. Each of those totems holds a soul prevented from entering Guinee. Since the magic is voodoo in origin, I can use this staff to focus your gathered music like a beacon into hell that only the spirits in the totems will hear. Once they latch onto the signal, you can pull them back to our reality."

At the entrance to the underground parking lot, Kendell stared up at the building. "Too bad Sanguine doesn't still have her wings. She could just fly the instruments up there."

Joe stood beside her. "I'm pretty sure I don't want to know what you're talking about. We'll figure out some way to get the elevators working."

Minerva's VW was parked alongside the solid metal door, which looked like it had come out of a World War II submarine. Polly stuck her head out of the side window. "Sounds like we finally get to do that gig up top while gazing out at the city."

Kendell inspected the back end of the van. It was stuffed with instruments and amplifiers. "All we have to do is lug all the equipment up to the top of the building. Stay here with the girls until we figure out a better solution."

Polly looked all too happy to leave the specifics of transportation to someone else. "Sanguine should be along any minute. She wanted to make a reconnaissance of the garage to make sure we weren't followed."

"Smart girl." Joe unlocked the door with some gadget out of his pack. The hatch opened with a whoosh as if the building had been deprived of air. Though the equipment was running as usual, the room was completely dark. Joe pulled out his military flashlight and began searching the room. "I kind of doubt this is going to take just turning on a light switch."

Sanguine stepped over the threshold and pulled the hatch shut. "If we're going to be at this for more than a minute, it might be best if we didn't advertise our presence."

Kendell stayed at Myles's side but addressed Sanguine. "If Colin is using magic to run this building, I guess it's up to us to figure out how to power up an elevator. You and I have spent the most time in hell. Any ideas?"

"You were alone with him up in his office. What did you see?"

Kendell squeezed Myles's hand. "Don't remind me. He had all kinds of control panels. You know, the old-school type with dials and levers and gauges. Nothing was computerized."

"Makes sense," Joe said. "This building was constructed

in the 1960s. Most of New Orleans hasn't been updated in a generation."

Myles could tell from the passing of the buck that no one had any ideas for getting upstairs. He turned to Kendell. "Tell the band to start bringing in the equipment. Joe and I can head up the stairs. There has to be an override among the motors and pulleys at the top of the building."

Joe headed to the stairwell. "Best idea I've heard so far. Good old-fashioned wrenching and jury-rigging. Now you're talking my kind of magic. Grab my pack."

Kendell pulled Myles into her arms. "Just be safe."

"Colin's in another dimension. I'll be fine."

"I meant, don't fall down the elevator shaft."

He chuckled. Physical danger in the real world hadn't been a worry in so long he'd forgotten about the typical warning. "Knowing Joe, he'll insist on taking on any dangerous aspect of this. Have everyone ready."

The paramilitary pack Joe carried with him hadn't looked that bad while they were on the street, but when Myles went to lift it, he nearly dislocated his shoulder. He handed it over as they began their climb. "What the hell have you got in this thing?"

"This and that. Think of it as a Boy Scout backpack on steroids. If we can't get the elevator working with what I've got, we'll at least be able to repel down the shaft."

The hike up the stairs winded Myles, but he didn't dare complain as he followed Joe, who was lugging his gear. They passed the entrance to the circular restaurant and continued to the elevator control room at the top of the building.

"I'm surprised this isn't sealed off with warning labels all over the place."

Joe pulled a small crowbar from his pack. "It's more secure than it looks. I broke into my fair share of rooftop control rooms as a kid." He shoved the sharpened end between the door and the frame and snapped the lock as if it were a toothpick.

"Jesus." Myles found the warning labels he'd expected. Red and yellow Danger High Voltage signs covered every surface. "I might be inclined to leave the jury-rigging to you."

"Check for a cabinet labeled Relays. It'll be the only one without a warning label. I'll need some heavy-gauge wire and any connectors you can find. Most of this equipment is to tell the elevators where to go. That back wall is the real fun part. We'll need a power source to tap into. Luther hates relying on outside sources of electricity, but he also believes in redundancy. Somewhere back there, you should find a steel cage marked 'City Power.' Don't open it."

Myles squeezed past the huge drums layered with steel cables. "No worries. I'm not touching a damn thing in here."

The spare parts cabinet was filled with boxes of electronic equipment from another era. "How do they even get replacement parts for this thing?"

"You're looking at it. When those run out, they pretty much have to find another old building to loot. Any luck finding some wire?"

At the bottom of the cabinet sat spools of wire in various colors. "Yep. I'll bring you the heaviest gauge before looking for the city's power."

When he got back, Joe had already pulled out the bottom and top relays and one partway down. The far bank of electronic equipment had the Danger sign removed. Seeing him there was like watching MacGyver in action.

"I figure we only need to go from the basement to the top floor," Joe said.

"What about that other one?"

He pointed at it with his wire cutters. "Luther's office. I can't do much for you once everyone's upstairs, so I thought I'd use that time to see if I could release Luther. In spite of Kendell's misgivings, he might come in handy."

Myles figured he, and everyone else, had given in to Kendell's positive assumptions about Delphine enough times to earn a little goodwill when it came to Luther. "How pissed do you think he'll be at Colin?"

"I'll let you know. I'm very curious about his reaction. Either he really is working with Colin—in which case, I'll see his alarm at me freeing him—or he'll prove to be our ace in the hole."

Myles set down the heavy spool. "What next?"

"Take these cutters and measure out some cable from that junction box to the city's power. Be generous in your measuring."

Myles had worked enough construction jobs in his time to know the drill. Unless a foreman was trying to save money, such jobs generally required fast-and-dirty work, and being too short with a measurement was a yelling offense.

By the time Joe had finished, the panel looked like a wall covered in spaghetti that had been thrown in a fit of rage.

"It's not pretty, but it should work. All the same, you might want to retreat to the stairwell when I throw the breaker."

Myles stood well back but within eyesight of Joe.

"Here goes nothing." Joe used a wooden broom handle to throw the huge lever. Sparks lit up the panel he'd been working on, but nothing caught fire. "Go down to the restaurant and the elevators. Use number three to go get the others. Maybe it would be good if you all came up together. I'll stay here and keep this running for as long as I can."

Myles ran down the stairs. The center elevator had its doors open. Gingerly, he hit the button for the basement. He held his breath for the whole ride down.

He barely waited for the doors to open. "Come on, everyone in. I'm not sure our fix has more than one lift in it."

∽

KENDELL HELPED SET up the equipment onstage. She needed every person present to make the magic happen, but she didn't have to like it. They'd all risked their necks too many times on her behalf. *Just once, it would be nice to take care of matters on my own.*

Myles set up a chair in front of the stage, facing away from the band, then plugged the equipment into the floor outlets. "You do what you do, and I'll do what I do. We'll call those lost souls out of hell."

Despite the fact that she wanted to keep him safe, his presence reassured her. "I'm sorry I've been such a pain. I don't know what's going on with me lately. When I listen to the words that come out of my mouth, I sound like Sanguine."

He gave her a kiss before taking his seat. "You've both spent way too much time in hell."

She returned to the stage and strapped on her black guitar before turning to the band. "I know it's not the loud, in-your-face music we usually play, but I want to go with 'Jar of Hearts.' Polly's sweet voice should do it justice."

As they began playing, Myles held his cane out to the side like a supernatural microphone. The green stone under the silver skull began to glow. Sanguine spun around the room like a temptress gypsy enticing the spirits from the beyond. Only Joe was missing from the gathering. Kendell assumed he was standing watch in some shadowy spot in case their breaking and entering should be discovered.

The eight blue-glass jars pulled at her soul. She pulled right back with her music. Polly's soft, lilting voice worked wonders at calming the distrusting spirits. Instead of materializing all across the room and roof, the eight totems lined up in front of Myles like schoolchildren treated to a class outing.

Once the song ended and all the voodoo totems were fully present, Kendell felt drained, but she was also exhilarated. The combination of her music and Myles's cane had created magic capable of combating Colin on his own turf. They'd won, and he'd lost—pure and simple.

Sanguine went to the totems and touched them as if making sure they were real. "Completely solid. Not a hologram in the bunch. Colin must be pissing nails right now."

Kendell really wished she could accept victory without the nagging doubt. "With his time standing still, he would have had plenty of opportunity to bust into our dimension. So why isn't he here?"

"He was trapped in one time, something like two months in our past," Sanguine said. "Like getting you through Guinee, he would have had to match up when he was with when we are now, and our time is a moving target. That's a lot to figure out. Personally, until I see otherwise, I'm taking these little wooden dudes as an indication we're finally one step ahead."

Kendell desperately hoped Sanguine was right and their victory wasn't just another misdirection from Colin. "If I've learned anything from chasing Colin, it's when he is ahead, he'll do everything he can to maintain that advantage. I've never seen him gloat in victory. We've stolen his ability to direct the paranormal power he's gathered, but he's still got all that energy right under our feet."

"Precisely so." Luther was standing by the elevator next to Joe. "I congratulate you on a clever victory. You've succeeded where I failed, but our villain is far from contained."

Kendell glared at Luther, then Joe, and finally at Myles. "I thought we weren't including him."

Myles didn't look in the least bit contrite. "Joe convinced me Luther would be more of an asset than a threat. His being held prisoner kind of tips the argument against him working for Colin."

Luther walked to the stage as if he owned the place, which, Kendell had to remind herself, he did. "I understand your misgivings. They are not unfounded. Colin, like Lincoln Laroque and Baron Malveaux before him, has been a generous contributor to the upkeep and expansion of this facility. That does not, however, give him the control he believes he's due. When he approached me about utilizing the objects in my care, I turned him down."

Kendell didn't find his argument convincing. "Then how did he gain control? He'd need to do more than just break in."

"The funny thing is, entering is the one concession I do grant him. He doesn't have free rein, of course, but anytime he wishes, he's welcome to meet with me. Apparently, even that small opening was all he needed."

"I think you owe us an explanation," Joe said.

"The guard station phone in the downstairs lobby hooks directly to my office—no matter the dimension. Embassies aren't much use if those inside them can't contact their home offices, so from the moment I heard Colin was banished to hell, I'd been expecting his call. Originally, he claimed to simply want the totems back. As he spent more time up here, we started arguing about his demand for access to the objects in my care. Finally, he acquiesced to only having use of this old restaurant. He explained the power here was better than what he had available in his office."

The explanation only slightly eased Kendell's suspicions. Colin had conned her plenty of times, but she wasn't a professional at chicanery like Luther. "And you couldn't tell what he was up to, or warned us? Hell, even Delphine could have been of use. These totems do belong to her. A little heads-up might have saved everyone a lot of hellish work."

"Once he established control up here, the first thing he did was completely cut me off. I couldn't even call my secretary. Which, as I thought about it, was kind of odd. She should have noticed something was wrong. We have procedures in place in case of attack. As she wasn't at her desk when Joe rescued me, I have to assume she was working with Colin. That man has a way with women."

Kendell went hot with anger. "He's a manipulative bastard who deserves his hell. You won't get any arguments from me on that point. You know what you've got here. What can he accomplish without the totems?"

"Quite a lot, I'm afraid. Though depriving him of his most obvious tools will send him back to the drawing board."

~

COLIN WAS certain his head was about to explode. He hadn't been this angry since the day he woke up in hell. Without anyone to yell at, however, he drove the anger down like the earth compressing coal into diamonds.

"Nicely played, little witch. I'll confess, I didn't see that one coming."

He stared around the empty room and rooftop. Without the totems, he had bigger problems than a guitar-playing girl with delusions of godlike powers. He didn't need to wait around to see that the sun had stopped moving across the sky. With his paranormal reactor, he'd managed to double the normal observation of time. A day took only twelve hours. Though he could have increased time's passage even further, he didn't dare overshoot Kendell's time frame.

Without the totems, however, all that lovely power had nowhere to vent. Every gauge related to energy storage was heading toward red.

He turned to the streetcar control panel and cranked up every car to full speed—a whopping ten miles per hour. The main power-generation gauge hardly noticed the increased demand.

"Fuck it." He returned to the main board and flipped off the limiters that regulated how much power went to any given city utility then ran to the windows to see his city in fast motion. At forty miles per hour, two of the streetcars jumped their tracks as they missed their turns. Decatur Street lit up like a Christmas tree just before blowing out half of its streetlights.

"Damn it!" He raced back to the main board and reinstituted the limiters.

Like a madman, he hunted around the panels for something else to power up. "Yes!" Though the hurricane was long gone, the pump stations were still online. Water was slowly being drained from the catch basins around the city. He cranked up the lumbering pumps to full capacity. So long as time remained at a standstill, there would be enough water in the system to prevent the old machinery from burning out.

He glanced back at his power supply. The building was still kicking out electricity like a runaway nuclear reactor, but the overall demand had slowed down the overheating of the storage units to something almost reasonable. "Hell won't be exploding today."

With the latest crisis averted, he turned back to the window. Late afternoon on a windless day wasn't the worst time to be stuck in, but Kendell and her cohorts would once again be slipping away into the future. He'd been so close he could taste victory, and that had made him careless. He glared at his pocket watch with the gold cufflink wired to the battery. As the minute hand moved, he could practically see her escaping his grasp. "I might have lost my fishing pole, but the hook is still set, and I'm still holding the reel."

He wasn't about to contemplate failure, but he needed a new plan. Kendell had come too close to discovering his last resort. Blowing hell to pieces would make for an interesting afterlife, but he wasn't ready to push the detonation button just yet.

A walk usually helped clear his head, especially after a near-death experience. He pushed the button for the elevator, expecting it to open immediately. When it didn't, he backed up to check the location needle that pointed to the basement. "So you weren't working alone, I see. I can't imagine any of your bandmates or that dolt of a boyfriend would have the first idea of how to hotwire an elevator. With Luther stashed away, that doesn't leave many people who might understand 1960s technology."

He pulled out the sheet of paper he kept in his pocket for recording his observations. So far, he had Kendell, her four fellow band members, Sanguine, and Myles as the core gang. Of their secondary helpers, only the lanky dude they called the professor seemed in any way mechanically oriented, but he didn't seem the type to risk his neck. Had Delphine been playing with her spells to free the elevator, she'd have encountered one of his fire wraiths hiding in the ceiling of the lift. That left only the dark question mark. Someone understood the workings of the World Trade Center, probably had military training, based on his stealth, and was good with tools.

He folded the page and put it back in his shirt pocket. He wasn't about to resort to climbing down the thirty-three stories. He grabbed his long coat and stepped out onto the roof. "Flying is a completely reasonable option."

9

*W*ith Myles making trips to Guinee, hell, and the *deep waters*—not to mention meeting interdimensional people and combating the devil himself —*normal* wasn't a word he often used when thinking about his life. As he sat next to Sanguine, listening to Polly Urethane and the Strippers practicing at the Scratchy Dog, he longed for the life that always seemed to be just beyond his grasp. Doughnut Hole sat at his side while Cheesecake lounged onstage like a drunk who had passed out at the singer's feet.

Sanguine leaned toward him. "It's going to be a great show tonight."

"They do seem to be playing really tight."

"No, you don't understand. I can see it. This place is going to be packed. You might want to have Charlie lay in a couple more cases of Abita Amber."

Her predictions had been right more often than not.

"I'll let him know. Have you got anything beyond how the night will play out?"

"Without insect vision, I'm at a loss for exact future sight. I get premonitions. Guess I should add *clairvoyant* to my list of job titles."

He had too much on his magical plate to feel envious. "Sounds confusing."

"More like disorienting. Like any other power, give me a couple of weeks, and the visions will seem like no big deal. I'm not kidding about that beer though."

He knew when a woman was giving him an order. "I'm on it."

Doughnut Hole followed along like an attentive assistant.

"How we looking, Charlie? Anything I can do?" Myles asked. Though he was co-owner, he would always view Charlie as the true manager of the club.

"With the house band once again sporting its lead guitarist, I'm expecting a big night. You free to pick up your usual gig?"

"I'll be slinging the bottles with you all night. Sanguine says we'll need a couple more cases of Abita Amber."

Charlie opened the beer fridge. "We look okay, but I'll grab a few more just to be sure. I wouldn't want to cross that sexy witch."

"How was Kendell's fill-in?"

Charlie leaned across the bar. "Let me tell you. Val Spar is no Olympia Stain. If you and Kendell's side gigs start getting any more distracting, Polly is going to have to do a search for a real guitarist. By the second night, our revenues were down by half."

"Trust me, brother, this distraction was hell. I'm just glad to see Kendell back onstage."

The band's playing grew so loud Charlie had to yell. "She's certainly playing with more intensity."

Myles knew the feeling of being infected with Baron Malveaux's energy. He'd been trapped in his own living hell while under the baron's possession—unable to express the rage that dominated every thought. Watching from the bar, Myles began to wonder if his sexy girlfriend behind the black guitar was channeling her Olympia Stain stage persona or if something darker was influencing her music.

He needed help. When it came to women and their moods, he had a near-perfect record for picking the wrong answer. "Any chance you've seen Delphine de Galpion recently?"

Charlie was double-checking his inventory sheet before making his final stocking run prior to opening. "I thought you didn't trust her."

"I don't, but she does have her uses. While you're out, think you could swing by her place and let her know I'd like to talk?"

"Yes, boss."

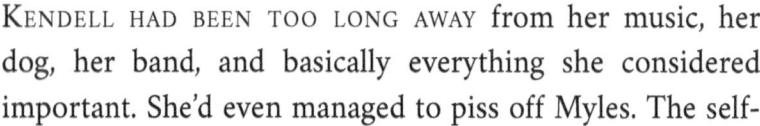

KENDELL HAD BEEN TOO LONG AWAY from her music, her dog, her band, and basically everything she considered important. She'd even managed to piss off Myles. The self-condemnation ran out her fingers and against the strings of her guitar as the band played their usual Friday night gig.

As hard as she tried, Colin kept creeping back into her thoughts, even while she was onstage. She held tightly to her anger toward him. The intense emotion drove her harder into No Doubt's "Just a Girl" than she had intended. By the end of the number, she needed a break.

She held the guitar toward Polly. "I need to change a string. It'll only take a minute."

"You have gotten pretty good at quick changes. I'll have the band play something mellow while you get fixed up." Polly stepped up to the microphone. "Any of you who've been around the last few weeks will recognize this one. I'm gonna grab myself a beer while I turn the band over to the rhythm section."

Kendell hadn't really expected the band to take five just because she needed to make the repair, but the ease with which they transitioned to playing without her gave her the chills. To her amazement, Minerva stepped out from behind her drum kit and took the microphone for "In the Cold, Cold Night." Scraper's bass accompaniment worked well with Minerva's deep, smoky voice, though Kendell wondered how the duo had originally convinced Polly to turn loose of the microphone. Kendell sat next to the lead singer at the bar and fixed her strings.

"They sound good," Myles said while mixing up margaritas for some college kids.

Polly had the look of a mother watching her kids' recital. "We had to get a little creative without a strong lead guitarist. Scraper is far more versatile on that bass than she lets on. Minerva's never going to be more than an oddity singer, but the chemistry between the two has a magical quality that draws in the crowd."

Kendell stopped feeding the steel string through the bridge of her guitar. "How long have I been gone, and since when have you been so savvy about crowd reactions?"

"Too long, and I never had to before. Don't get me wrong. We miss you like crazy, but any other guitarist would be out on her ass if she left us high and dry. You're family, and I get why you've gotta do what you've gotta do. You being gone, however, has meant each of us had to up our game. Even so, the girls still voted me off guitar."

Kendell went back to fixing her ax but kept her eyes on Polly. "Sounds to me like you've upped your leadership role. If I'm not careful, you're going to turn this group into something famous."

Polly shrugged. "Would that be so bad, Miss Business Owner? A versatile house band might just earn this club the reputation it deserves on Frenchmen Street."

Kendell finished tuning the strings to the best of her ability without an amp. "Let's get back up there before Scraper and Minerva rename us the Black Stripes."

She felt much more connected to the band during the second half of the gig. The ghost of Colin Malveaux might threaten her thoughts, but music was Kendell's personal dimension. She was the one to decide if he was welcome in her mental audience.

Each of her bandmates gave her huge hugs at the end of the last number. All five of them linked arms over shoulders for their final acknowledgement of the applause.

The job of Olympia Stain the musician might have ended, but Kendell Summer the bar owner still had to help close up the club. Myles had looked worried most of the night. His actions weren't obvious enough to be noticeable by any drunk customer, but as his partner and lover, Kendell caught every furrowed brow as he looked to the stage. While Charlie did his final inventory, she grabbed a couple of beers and hustled Myles out back.

"You don't have to worry about me every time I have a killer performance."

He took the offered bottle and sat at the metal table. "You remember how we talked about you keeping an eye on me for any change in personality after the baron took control my body?"

As if she was ever going to forget her part in his possession. "Of course, but I'm not feeling anything off about you. Are you worried about the cane?"

He opened her beer and set it across the table. "I'm not worried about something happening to me. I've been discounting your moods to spending too much time in hell. Both you and Sanguine haven't been yourselves. In her case, I get it. Being a fallen angel who no longer has her wings or the ability to see clearly into the future must make this reality feel like hell. I'm more worried about you."

Her natural reaction was to defend herself, but the agreement to listen worked both ways. They'd subjected themselves, and each other, to too many threats for her to be belligerent. "What do you propose?"

Instead of being relieved at her acceptance as she'd hoped, he stared at his beer. "When it comes to matters involving voodoo, I only trust Delphine to do what's in the best interest of her family's history. When it comes to you, however, I do believe she sees you as a protégée and a friend."

A cold fear whose source she couldn't identify gripped Kendell's heart. "What do you think she can do?"

Myles downed a good portion of his beer. "If you're being influenced from hell, she should be able to identify the source."

"You think Colin has some kind of handle on me?" She tried not to make the question come out as a challenge, but even to her, the words sounded confrontational.

"I think both you and Sanguine spent a lot of time in Colin's realm. Maybe the influence isn't from him. Sanguine said you two are the primary sources for what keeps that hell together. Even with the seven gates we built, and relieving you of some of that responsibility for Colin, maybe your soul needs a break."

"And are you proposing we bring Sanguine along to Delphine's inspection?" *Good luck with that.*

He toyed with his empty beer bottle. "You are my first priority. I won't even go with you if you don't want me present. I'm just worried about you, Kendell. You're snappish toward me, cut me out of your plans, and play onstage like you're up there all alone."

She looked at him in shock. "I was fully a part of the band tonight. You've got no right to judge my playing."

"Of the two of us, you've always been far more analytical. Tell me something hasn't changed. I'm going to grab a couple more beers while you think about it."

Being left alone deprived her of an adversary, and that meant she had to face herself. She had been more on edge lately. The characteristics that Myles had described had bugged the hell out of her when she'd noticed them in Sanguine. People were no longer like interesting books Kendell wanted to delve into but obstacles she had to work around. No one understood. Her temper didn't want to be placated but challenged. Maybe Sanguine wasn't just playing the bratty younger sibling. Maybe she had been influenced by her grandmother's creation. And if Sanguine had been affected, that meant Kendell had to accept the same diagnosis.

By the time Myles returned with the beers, she understood how much pain she'd caused him. "I'll go see Delphine, and I'll bring Sanguine with me. Though it might be better if you asked her. In spite of her snarkiness, she does like you. She sees me too much like a sister to take me seriously enough to listen to. Plus, you're the one who is seeing the change."

Myles drank his beer. "I don't have a problem setting up the meeting."

"I don't want to hide anything from you, but it might be best if you didn't come along. Even though she'll listen to you, Sanguine can be pretty difficult when she feels cornered and outnumbered. Women can be pretty defensive when being poked and prodded, especially when it comes to our souls."

~

Sanguine knew she was being played. Myles just never was all that clever. But he had a point about Kendell acting oddly. Meeting her and Delphine for lunch brought back memories of figuring out how to break into hell. Sanguine had won that debate. The victory gave her confidence to again meet with the voodoo priestess.

She got to the café first and ordered a Sazerac. The absinthe mellowed with rye and given a little zing with bitters reminded her of working up potions under her grandmother's watchful, though blind, eye. Not everything about New Orleans sucked, just the people.

Kendell looked as though she hadn't slept in days as she entered the courtyard, but she perked up on making eye contact with Sanguine. "I thought Delphine would have beaten us. She likes being able to set up her little tricks before the marks show up."

Sanguine had trouble believing the words of judgment had come from Kendell. They sounded more like something Sanguine herself would say. "It's just us for the moment. You should try their Sazeracs. They're very good."

"No, thanks. Ever since Myles said he'd make one for Colin should he pass Myles's fifth gate, I've sworn off them. Has he explained to you that he thinks we've got some plague from hell?"

Sanguine motioned to the waitress for another drink and to take Kendell's order. With their drinks secured, she sat back to enjoy the sun. "That boyfriend of yours worries too much. Sure, the energy from hell interacts with who we are—that's inevitable—but it's not like we change into demons."

Kendell had the slow deliberation Myles often displayed when he didn't like an answer. "So you're saying he's right?"

"It's not like the devil has your soul. Actually, it's kind of the opposite. You know why I hate being in relationships?"

"What does your fear of commitment have to do with anything?" Kendell asked.

"I'm trying to illustrate my point. When I'm seeing someone, I feel like I lose a part of myself to them. There's a melding of spirits, and I don't like it. I'm me, and that's the way it should stay."

"What does that have to do with being infected by hell?"

Sanguine wondered how Kendell could be so dense sometimes. She sighed heavily at having to explain the obvious. "Agnes built this hell. You know that. When she died, she willed it to us. And by willed, I don't mean we inherited it. Her force of will bonded us together." She grabbed a salt shaker and closed her hands around it as a visual representation. "Our combined energy is what holds Colin in place. But you already know that too." The final cut was as close to a slap in Kendell's face as Sanguine dared.

"You've explained some of that before. Are you saying you and I are in something like a romantic relationship? Just don't tell me we're in a threesome with Colin."

Kendell's naivety reminded Sanguine of a virgin who didn't know if going to third base constituted sex or not.

"Of course not. Don't be ridiculous. If you and I were in love, you'd know it. I'm not one of those women who plays coy or hard to get."

Kendell practically snatched her mimosa out of the waitress's hand. She then proceeded to just sit there, drink in hand, until the woman left. "I didn't say we were in love," she whispered. "I said *like* a romantic relationship."

Sanguine did her best not to laugh at her friend. "Your repression is duly noted, my straight friend."

Delphine arrived before Sanguine had a chance to further embarrass Kendell. "Sorry I'm late. Myles's descriptions of what he thinks he's noticed had me delve deeper into Marie's journals than I'd planned."

Kendell finally set down her mimosa. "How is your library?"

"Now that you've returned my totems and journals, I've been busy putting things back where they belong." Delphine motioned to the waitress and ordered a white wine.

Sanguine wondered if Delphine kept any kind of an inventory. "Have you noticed anything else missing?"

Delphine nodded. "My shop may be an embassy in hell, but it's not as secure as, say, the World Trade Center. Luther got to dictate what Colin could do in his building, but as the one who originally cast the Malveaux curse, Marie didn't bother with a similar paranormal security system. Things come and go out of my shop with disconcerting regularity. It's more like an interdimensional lending library without a way of keeping tabs on the borrowers."

Sanguine wished her Sazerac were a double. "That doesn't sound very safe."

"The only spirits with access are supposed to be members of fellow embassies. As Colin is the only person in his realm, and he thinks of himself as the devil, I suspect he found a loophole in the charter."

The way Kendell grasped her glass made Sanguine wonder why the thing didn't explode into a million pieces.

"So just to get this over with, are we possessed by the devil?" Kendell asked.

Delphine pulled out two candles from her bag and lit one next to each woman. The scent of vanilla didn't mix well with Sanguine's Sazerac. "I doubt you're under Colin's possession. He's in his hell, and possession kind of requires one spirit to inhabit another's body. Under his control would be another story, but again, with him so isolated, I can't see that as being possible either."

Sanguine could practically hear Kendell sigh with relief. "So Myles was wrong."

"Don't sound so pleased," Delphine said. "Possession and control are easily diagnosed and dealt with. If Colin is somehow affecting your thoughts and actions, there's something else going on—something that shouldn't be possible, considering his isolation from this reality. Tell me, did either of you bring back any mementoes from hell?"

Sanguine couldn't contain her laughter. "Why in hell would we bring anything back? We did retrieve your voodoo dolls from on top of the World Trade Center, if they count. But we weren't in hell at the time."

"Those totems belong in this realm. Everything in my library eventually finds its way home. His connection would be more personal."

Sanguine honestly didn't care about Delphine's belongings. The inner workings of voodoo held all the appeal of a college calculus class. "So long as those aren't what you were talking about, we should be fine."

Kendell looked like a girl who'd just been caught stealing diamond earrings from her mother's purse. She pulled a gold cufflink from her pocket and set it in front of Delphine. The candle flames next to both women moved toward the piece of jewelry as though someone were squirting them with lighter fluid.

"Colin said we could talk over the two cufflinks like tin cans on a string."

"And you fucking believed him?" Sanguine couldn't hold in her anger. "After all we've been through, you have got to be the most—"

"Enough!" Delphine cut in. "There's no point in assigning blame."

Sanguine agreed that there was no point searching for a guilty party when a confession was literally on the table. "She's given him an opening!"

"What's done is done," Delphine said, showing that she was only slightly less naïve than Kendell. "At least we now know how he's infecting you with his emotions. The question now is, how do we turn this to our favor? Why did he think it would be useful to talk to you?"

Sanguine cut off Kendell before she could answer. "And why in the name of all that's holy did you want to talk to him?"

Kendell sat straighter in her chair. "Because he had a point. You tossed him into hell without talking to me first. He isn't the only manipulative bastard I've had to deal with lately. I never asked to be a part of your grandmother's hell. There seem to be a lot of assumptions in the Wiccan realm about what I'll accept. I'm no fan of Colin, but he isn't

Baron Malveaux. Lincoln Laroque might have been an asshole, but I've dealt with my fair share of arrogant pricks. They aren't all devils. Colin Malveaux shouldn't be convicted for Baron Malveaux's sins."

"They're one and the same," Sanguine said. "Do we really have to rehash the past?"

"He's only partly Baron Malveaux. My point is, this is a discussion that never took place. I was not Colin's judge, jury, or executioner—merely his jailor. If I'm to be held accountable for his incarceration, I deserve better than to be cut out of sentencing. He wanted to plead his case, and if I was to be responsible for his judgment, I figured he deserved his day before me."

The only thing Sanguine hated more than being questioned about her motives was being proven wrong by someone she cared about. "I didn't mean to cut you out of the decision to cast him into hell. I simply didn't want you to have to shoulder that burden. Agnes had her plan for Baron Malveaux in place long before either of us was born. But what do you intend to do—pardon him?"

"I'm not that foolish. When I trap a rattlesnake under a bucket, I don't let him out, hoping he'll be grateful to be freed. No matter which direction Colin would strike, it would be against someone I love."

Delphine put down her wine. "And he'd strike with supernatural powers. We have no way of knowing how much of what he's learned would transfer into our reality."

Sanguine still had phantom back spasms from her missing wings. "If I'm any indication, not as much as he might expect."

"You can see into the future. With time, the skills you learned in hell will become more apparent." Kendell gave a look of pity that only made Sanguine more furious at her for having accepted the cufflink.

"My point is," Sanguine said, repressing the desire to lash out, "he won't be able to spread his coat and fly or command the animals to do his bidding."

"Once again," Delphine said, "we're speculating on what may or may not happen if Colin finds a way out of hell, and that's not why you invited me to lunch. The golden cufflink gives Colin a tangible connection to our reality. He can't jump through it or use its cursed abilities to kill someone or anything like that. It's simply a road marker for him. The fact that it does carry the Malveaux curse and that—despite what Baron Samedi said—Kendell will always be connected to the curse means she is able to read his emotions." Delphine put her hand on Kendell's. "The only thing he can do is influence your emotions. Learn to identify what you're feeling and look for the cause. If you can't find one, the reaction is probably from Colin."

Sanguine wished her emotions were so easily identified, but Delphine's explanation seemed to calm Kendell. "So that's it? She hangs onto the golden cufflink like nothing's happened? Please don't tell me we're just being emotional, like some boyfriend discounting our feelings as hormones. If our problems are being caused by that cufflink, can't we stick it in a lead-lined box or something?"

Kendell piped in like a kid who thought she'd discovered the answer. "Like those metal-lined bags you used when I first brought you the cursed items."

"I can supply you with an isolation bag, but realize you'll be cutting off your connection to Colin. So long as he thinks he is in charge, you can lead him where you want him to go. Cut off the connection, and you lose a tactical advantage."

Sanguine couldn't take it any longer. "You sound exactly like Baron Samedi when it came to building the seven gates. Why is it always someone not in the line of fire who thinks they know best what we should do? I've been the bait used to attract Colin before. That didn't work out so well. He left me no choice but to cast him into hell. All this calm talk about how he was somehow condemned is bullshit. I was acting in self-preservation, for all of us. He would have taken Baron Samedi's cane. Then where would we be?"

Kendell passed the cufflink to Sanguine. "He did manipulate us both. Maybe you should be the one to decide what we do with his possession."

She picked it up and turned it in the light. "If we secure it, he'll know we've discovered his ploy, but he will lose his connection to us and our reality. This stupid little piece of gold is what he'd use as a homing device to figure out our time relative to when he's stuck. What we really need is to move this in time so he can't reach us, while making it look like Kendell still has the item with her."

Delphine pushed her wineglass aside. "There might be a way, but it would be complicated and dangerous. Voodoo totems hold the essence of a person in their spirit jars. First, I would need to harvest a piece of Kendell's soul. Next, I'd put it in a fetish along with the cufflink. Finally, we'd have

Myles deposit the sculpture in a parallel dimension by use of his cane. It might be enough to throw Colin off track."

"You have got to be fucking kidding me." Sanguine looked around the courtyard to make sure no one had noticed her outburst. She resumed her opposition in more modulated tones. "There is no way you're carving into Kendell's soul like a Thanksgiving turkey and tossing it into another dimension, hoping Colin follows it like a hungry dog."

"I'm merely suggesting options."

Delphine talking about options sounded too much like a mad scientist eager to play with her equipment, but Sanguine knew her own views on the subject were modest compared to those of the person who really mattered.

"Myles would cast *you* into another dimension if he was sitting here." She turned to Kendell. "We'll figure out something else. Your dog, boyfriend, and band need every part of your soul—as do I."

Kendell kept looking back at the cufflink. "I know you're right. All we seem to come up with, though, are last-resort options."

10

*M*yles did his best to sit quietly while Kendell and Sanguine reported on their lunch with Delphine. Neither Cheesecake nor Doughnut Hole did as well at keeping their emotions in check. Each time Delphine's name was mentioned, they both started growling their objections.

When Kendell explained the voodoo priestess's plan for dividing Kendell's soul, even Myles lost it. "And you just sat there, listening to this madness?"

Sanguine flapped her arms as if they were replacements for her wings. "That woman is barking mad. I nearly pulled Kendell right out of the restaurant. Don't worry, I gave Delphine a piece of my mind."

Kendell reached over and took Cheesecake into her arms. "It was just an idea. What if, instead of a piece of my soul, we could make, like, a mirror of me?"

"Sure," Sanguine shouted. "We'll just put a spell on your

compact and put *that* in the voodoo doll. Then when he does break into the secret realm, he'll have a mirror to watch your every movement. Do you honestly believe that's any less dangerous than what we have now?"

Though Myles agreed with Sanguine, he thought she didn't have to be so mean. "Kendell's idea could work as a starting point, as, I assume, Delphine meant hers to be. I can't believe she would really consider harvesting a piece of Kendell's soul."

Sanguine crossed her arms over her chest. Myles could just imagine how her wings would still be quivering in consternation. "You weren't there. She was deadly serious. Had I not been so adamant in my objection, we might all be standing in her voodoo surgical clinic right now."

Kendell struck back with such force even Cheesecake looked shocked. "I would never agree to anything she said without discussing it with Myles first. Look around this room. Do you really believe I'd let any of this love go? I hang onto those I care about with every aspect of my being. I would never leave."

He'd never heard her express her love so forcefully about anyone other than Cheesecake.

"Delphine has an abrupt way of presenting her ideas, and I don't trust her," Myles said. "I do appreciate Sanguine's concern that your idea could too easily lead Colin right back here. He's making bold moves to escape hell. We have to be ready for him. We all know his attraction to you. A voodoo doll in your likeness could too easily give him power over you. I feel like there is an answer, but it's just beyond my reach."

She snuggled next to him. Even Doughnut Hole calmed down. "We need a fake version of my soul that can be put in a voodoo totem and delivered to another dimension. The copy of me has to be convincing enough to fool Colin. Delphine can't make the copy, partly because of her lack of skill and partly because we'd never be sure of her loyalties. Just for a moment, let's put the copy of me aside. Where would you hide it?"

He preferred to deal with one problem at a time, but talking with Kendell had proved there was often a back door to the answer if he followed her lead. "The ideal dimension would be Colin's hell. He'd just end up doubling back to where he started."

Sanguine finally sat down. "You've already proven your skills at sneaking us into hell. I'm sure I could find a reasonable hiding time and place."

Kendell sat up. "It took too much work to get you *out* of hell. There's no way I'm letting you use my boyfriend to walk, or fly, back into your grandmother's reality."

"You still think I want to kill him, don't you?"

Myles could feel the argument brewing, but some disagreements need airing out. He didn't interrupt as Kendell got fired up.

"Tell me that's not still your plan," she said.

"So what's your option?" Sanguine asked. "You're not going back. Another conversation, and Colin will have you as his personal *escort* out of hell."

Letting them talk it out was one thing, but the implication of Kendell as Colin's sex servant was where Myles drew the line. "This isn't getting us anywhere.

Sanguine, just for the sake of argument, what would happen if Colin did circle back into his own hell but at a different time? If he breaks out, we're talking about the release of a lot of energy."

She closed her eyes as if she were trying to envision the event. "If the energy he expels isn't controlled, and the World Trade Center continues to build up power, it would be like a nuclear bomb setting off another nuclear bomb—a feedback of explosions that couldn't be contained in my grandmother's creation. We'd be looking at a catastrophic failure that would spread across dimensions. Colin the devil would rival Papa Ghede for supreme ruler, only instead of someone looking to create equals, we'd have, well, Colin."

"Good to know. So no hiding Kendell's spirit voodoo doll in hell. Someone should make a note of that."

Kendell held Cheesecake more tightly. "No need. That's not an image I'm likely to forget."

Myles tried to identify the other options. "Guinee is out. He's already done enough damage as Baron Samedi's replacement at the seventh gate. Plus, he's got too many allies there."

Sanguine bobbed her head as she thought. "My grandmother spent her whole life building that hell. Dimensions don't spring up overnight. And I'm not about to subject the people of some other realm to his treachery. We just might be able to use her hell if it was modified first. Her dimension needs to be able to handle the energy buildup. The big challenge would be finding a way for me to talk to my grandmother while she was still doing the construction. The second thing we'd need is a way to siphon off the World Trade Center power just as he detonates his bomb."

"Damn it." Myles got up so he could pace and think. "We need help. Someone who has experience with the beyond who isn't connected to voodoo. As I see it, there are two options. Luther Noire is no fan of Colin, but Colin has already bested Luther, so I'm not sure how much I'd trust his help. As for the other option, the sisters at Our Lady of Mercy don't have a very high regard for any of us, but I can't think of anyone more knowledgeable at dealing with the devil than the Catholic Church."

Sanguine shook her head so nervously Myles wondered if she realized what she was doing. "My grandmother warned me about those nuns. If you intend on consulting the Church, I'm out. The only reason they'd let me in the front door would be to burn me at the stake in their courtyard. I was only able to help last time because I was in Colin's hell. I expect they thought I was just another lost soul when I bashed at their door. I'm sorry. I love you, Kendell, but if he's serious, you're on your own."

Kendell set Cheesecake on the ottoman. "There are other ways into the church than the cloistered nunnery. We sent Professor Yates to Saint Louis Cathedral as our failsafe when we called forth Delphine's totems from Colin's hell. Maybe it's time we found out how he got along with the head of the diocese."

~

<small>THOUGH IT HAD BEEN</small> his idea, Myles had never had much

interaction with the Church. Like keeping his distance from a beehive on the path home from school, he had done his best to avoid any confrontation. Fortunately, that was what friends were for.

Professor Yates was busy cleaning out his bicycle-driven, gypsy-fortune-teller trailer when Myles and Kendell caught up to him at his office on the wharf. "What kind of mischief have you two gotten yourselves involved in this time?"

Myles pulled at one of the wood-spoke wheels, which felt too flimsy for the wagon. "You know, just the usual."

"That bad? And you're turning to me for help?"

"Hopefully, just an introduction," Kendell said. "How well do you get along with the Catholic Church?"

The lanky gentleman went back to pulling equipment out of the back of the wagon. "You really had no idea, did you? When you sent me to the cathedral to man the failsafe, it was just dumb luck that I happened to *be* Catholic. You know, anyone else would have just been laughed out of the sanctuary. Crazy old man walks in from Jackson Square, looking like a busker and talking about paranormal objects in an abandoned building—not exactly someone a member of the clergy is likely to listen to, even in confession."

Myles knew they'd asked a lot of the professor. "I should apologize for taking you for granted, but apparently, we take everyone for granted."

Professor Yates dropped a big box of electronic parts inside his office. "I just wanted to hear you say it. Father Carl and I go way back. We went to high school together. Even he had trouble getting the specifics of the failsafe from the bishop."

The fall breeze off the river felt good after the long, hot summer.

"I thought all you'd have to do was mention Luther Noire."

"There are some things one doesn't discuss inside the walls of the church. Luther and his organization are at the top of the list. Now, if you're not going to get to the point, mind helping me with this equipment?"

Myles felt stupid for not offering. "Of course. What are you doing anyway?"

"Fall cleaning. Getting ready for the Halloween rush. People who want to be scared don't want my readings to look overly scientific."

Myles climbed into the back of the wooden compartment and handed a pile of textbooks to Kendell. "We need to meet with someone about sending Colin to hell."

Professor Yates dropped the toolbox he'd been carrying. "You mean actual hell? Not just the made-up dimension your Wiccan swamp witch devised, but fire and brimstone, Beelzebub, Hades?"

Kendell walked past the awestruck gentleman. "That would be the one."

"Suddenly, I see why you didn't consider the fact that I found the failsafe to destroying those supernatural objects all that noteworthy. You know, the Church takes a pretty hard line on realms like heaven and hell. Father Carl calls himself a foot soldier for God. You're looking for a four-star general."

Myles found a broom at the front of the wagon and

started cleaning the rat turds from front corners. "I may have overstated our desires. If Colin finds a way out of his hell, which is sounding more likely with each passing contact, we'll need a way to combat him. Another dimension would be ideal, but barring that, it'd be nice to understand a little better how theirs works."

Kendell checked around the wagon for any housekeeping chores that had been missed. "Comparing notes might be the best description. We've got a problem with our hell and thought the Church might be willing to help. Does that sound better than us wanting to throw our trash out in their dumpster?"

Professor Yates closed up his office. "I can set up the appointment. I'll talk to Father Carl to see how high up the chain of command he can summon forth. Don't get your hopes up. Best you can realistically expect is a church-school lesson on the differences between heaven and hell or the seven deadly sins."

∽

KENDELL WAS RELIEVED Professor Yates wasn't directing them to the cathedral, or worse, the convent. But as she and Myles followed the professor into the boarded-up building on Conti Street with a bar on one side and a junk shop on the other, she wondered what they'd gotten into. The empty ground floor didn't inspire confidence.

"I realize the Church doesn't want to discuss issues involving the paranormal in their sanctuaries, but this feels like walking into the Spanish Inquisition."

Professor Yates unlocked a side door. "I spent the better part of yesterday afternoon convincing Father Carl I wasn't crazy. He accused me of spending too much time working the crowd around Jackson Square with the other fortune-tellers. I don't know what finally convinced him, but when I got home, I found an envelope with this key and instructions to bring you two. The note wasn't from my friend. After all these years, I know his handwriting as well as my own." The tall man had to duck under the angled roof of the stairwell as he climbed the creaking steps to the second floor.

Kendell's impression of the first floor was nothing compared to her fear of the upstairs. The wide-planked wooden floor had been painted black. She couldn't make out the walls and ceiling as the windows were covered in green paint. From the dried brushstrokes that extended across the glass, she assumed the supposed careless paint job had been intentional. An overhead bare light bulb illuminated a heavy oak desk that looked out of place in the run-down building.

She took the center of the three chairs, hoping having Myles and the professor on either side would give her comfort. It was only after they'd gotten comfortable that a man in black robes stepped out of the shadows. "You have questions. I'll answer what I can. There are rules. You're not to record our conversation, even on paper. Never return to this building. Do not attempt to contact me again. Understood?"

Myles took her hand under the desk. "We understand. Who are you?"

"You can call me Brother Aramis." He sat at the other side of the antique table and opened a journal that half covered the desktop. "You were inquiring about Archibald Baptiste Malveaux."

Kendell wasn't interested in rehashing history. "Actually, we're concerned about Colin Malveaux. Archibald was his great-grandfather."

"One step at a time." The man sounded unimpressed by her knowledge of Colin's past. "Archibald Malveaux was a generous contributor to our diocese." He looked up at her from under the cowl of his robes. The glare off his reading glasses prevented her from seeing his eyes. "The baron, you see, believed in covering his bets."

Kendell wondered if the disclosure was meant as a threat or as an admission. "So you work for him too?"

"No. I tell you of his patronage so you'll understand our position and why I'm talking to you now." He tapped the yellowed page of the suede-covered book. "We keep close track of our parishioners. Archibald Malveaux had many flaws when it came to being a Christian, but so long as he repented on Sunday, we overlooked his whorehouses and questionable business dealings conducted during the workweek."

Kendell's impression of the Church wasn't improving in the least. "You mean so long as he kept your coffers filled."

The man laced his fingers together and put them to his mouth like a school principal trying to decide on an appropriate punishment. "The Catholic Church appreciates the help of well-to-do citizens such as the Malveauxs, but we are beholden to no one but God."

Myles squeezed her hand, indicating he hoped to avoid an argument. "If he was so well regarded, why did you agree to meet with us?"

"We could overlook his misdeeds. All of us are sinners. But when he accepted the voodoo cane and started calling himself Baron Malveaux—rightful heir to Baron Samedi—we were left with no choice but excommunication. This is where the Church and Marie Laveau crossed paths. Catholicism and voodoo have had a long history of interaction. Many of the voodoo beliefs and loas were derived from our sacraments and saints, though who was the originator and who the imitator depends on which faith you're talking to at the moment."

"She came to you for help, and you did nothing?" Kendell asked. Myles would have been more diplomatic, but sometimes being polite got in the way of finding answers.

"I said we had interactions. The Church isn't here to accept the rejects of failed false religions, and Marie wasn't the type to pawn off her mistakes on others. Like you, she wanted information on hell."

Kendell leaned forward and tried to make out what was written in the ledger. "You're saying she and Agnes Delarosa fashioned Colin's hell on your actual afterlife realm? What does your book say happened?" The words weren't in English. From the age and source, she assumed they were Latin.

"We don't build realms. Heaven and hell are the purview of God Almighty. Man's job on earth is to discover the will of the divine, not attempt to copy Him."

She leaned back so Myles could lead the conversation.

"She didn't mean to offend, but you must realize what we're up against."

The shadowy man nodded and returned to his ledger. "Baron Malveaux ended up being the wedge that forced voodoo and the Church apart. Though Madam Laveau attempted to limit his access to the dark arts, Archibald managed to subvert her authority within the voodoo tradition. For a time, even the loas of the dead bowed down to him."

"Wait," Myles said. "How much do you know about the loas of the dead? Even I didn't realize he had achieved that much power in Guinee. I thought he only managed to rule the seventh gate."

"The Church would be foolish to only focus on what we teach our congregations. Keeping an eye on the other belief systems, though it's not outwardly acknowledged, has been our mandate from the time of Christ. We could hardly convince members of false religions to join us if we didn't first understand where they'd gone wrong and what they'd gotten right."

Professor Yates rubbed at his scraggly beard, a motion that meant he'd hit on something significant. "I remember talking to Father Carl about how the Church often absorbed ceremonies from pagan cultures in order to entice their people to convert. How far do you personally pursue these ideas?"

"You're asking if I believe in voodoo's ideas about Guinee, the loas, and the *deep waters*, I see a lot of crossover. Often our disagreements are more matters of semantics than real differences."

Kendell could see the rest of the afternoon veering off into speculation about philosophies if left to the two old men. "So you have no allegiance to Baron Malveaux even though he did contribute to the church, and your uneasy alliance with voodoo prevents you from going into details about what was discussed with Marie Laveau. Can we get to Colin now?"

He consulted a computer tablet off to the side of the desk. "For someone so enamored with books, you don't seem to care for character buildup, Miss Summer."

It took all of her inner strength to remain seated. "You drive your point home with all the subtlety of a jackhammer. I get it. You keep track of me just like you did with Archibald Malveaux—though, in place of a dusty journal, you've updated your method of recording information."

Myles again tried to steer a neutral course through the conversation. "Once you excommunicated the baron, what was your interaction with the Malveaux family? His son, for instance, never embraced voodoo, and the baron's wife ended her days in Our Lady of Mercy Convent."

"We looked after Miss Fleur with all the love someone would have for a favorite aunt who'd endured an abusive marriage. If anyone could have convinced the Church to act against Baron Malveaux, it would have been Fleurentine Laurette-Malveaux. Fortunately for us, she never asked. As for Antoine Laurette, we offered our services, but he refused."

Kendell wondered whether the monk's stern reaction toward her was because she was a woman, or if she just got under his skin by not taking everything he said as gospel. "Then you know of the cursed objects," she said, not wanting to leave all the questions to Myles. "But my understanding is the Church doesn't deal with supernaturally charged items, only those belonging to the saints."

"It must be obvious that if we had dealings with Marie Laveau, we would also be aware of Luther Noire's operation. He's proven useful in safeguarding certain items we'd rather not have in our possession. But again, Antoine wasn't interested in abdicating his family responsibility."

Myles let go of Kendell's hand and leaned on the desk. "I think we have a pretty clear understanding of the Church's relationship to Archibald. What about the other half of Colin—Lincoln Laroque?"

Brother Aramis turned the pages slowly as if following the family line's century-old interaction with the Church. "Between Archibald and Lincoln, the family may have changed names, but their patronage of the Catholic Church remained unblemished."

Kendell began to wonder if the man under the hood really believed money didn't buy loyalty. "With a family that rich and powerful, I'd guess their contributions have done a lot toward building the diocese to what it is today."

He rested his hands on the pages as if he was about to lunge across the desk. "As I've told you, money is only a means to an end for the Church. We are not for sale, no matter the bidder."

"I didn't mean to impugn your integrity, but how open would you be if our questions were just regarding an average family and not the most powerful people in New Orleans?"

He leaned back into his chair. "Had Professor Yates not asked about Baron Malveaux, we wouldn't even be meeting. If you'll allow me to continue, perhaps you'll learn why."

Kendell was suddenly grateful to have been educated in the public schools and not under the direction of the Church. "I'll just sit here quietly minding my manners then."

He returned to the book as if her answer wasn't meant to be sarcastic. "Like his ancestor, Lincoln Laroque was a fan of covering his bets. Though not brought up a Catholic, his contributions have been sizable and without expectations." He looked up over his reading glasses. "We have been expecting some request from him, but so far, he seems content to believe he has us in his debt should the need arise."

Kendell was happy to let Myles be the one to skate out onto the thin ice. "Are you aware of how Lincoln became Colin?"

"And now we get to the crux of the matter." Brother Aramis closed the massive ledger. "For some topics, the Church still believes in an oral tradition. A story, once written, loses the dynamic flow of the spoken word. So it is with the creations of devils and saints. Once the facts are laid bare for all to see, the Church sanctifies the work of people like me. Until that day, however, I'm bound to my predecessors through our evolving understanding of the facts."

Myles nodded as if what Brother Aramis said made perfect sense. "Baron Malveaux found his way out of

Guinee. He possessed my body, driving my soul into a dark corner I'd rather not discuss. He was exorcised out of me and into a voodoo spirit jar. Lincoln drank the liquid essence and became Colin Malveaux."

Brother Aramis took in the information in silence. His blank expression reminded Kendell of a computer's lack of emotion as data was fed into it. "Is this where Sanguine Delarosa enters the story?"

Kendell sensed her swamp witch friend was about to be condemned by the Church. "She's not responsible for what her grandmother created. Sanguine was only trying to protect the living from what Colin had become."

Brother Aramis crossed his arms over the book and closed his eyes. "Emotions are one of the experiences we try to remove from the retelling of a story. Though your passion for your friend is admirable, it's of little use in finding your answer."

Myles put his hand on her knee, and she remained quiet, letting him take the lead. "If you remove emotion, you remove all understanding of Sanguine Delarosa. In her world, love overrides logic. We came here today because we wanted to understand not what your church preaches, but what it does. What we believe about forgiveness, the bonding of human spirits, and an understanding of who we truly are is only getting in the way of us containing Colin. You're the expert on separating people into the saved and the damned."

Kendell had never wanted to kiss Myles more, but this was hardly the time and place. "Agnes Delarosa based

Colin's hell at least in part on what your church has spent the last millennia describing. Where did we go wrong?"

"Pure evil will find its natural state, but we don't believe any person is fully good or bad. A spirit that sees itself as unredeemable gratefully accepts banishment. Satan, the fallen angel, doesn't hate hell. It is his domain. Those unfortunates banished to his realm might wish for redemption, but he does not. This simple distinction is how you will know if Colin is your devil ruling his domain, or a spirit forced there against his will."

For once, Kendell hoped Colin really was the devil. "I can't image anyone more evil in thoughts and deeds than Baron Malveaux, but I can't answer for Colin."

"Our hell wasn't created by humanity, with its mixture of good and evil, nor does God rule over hell. Evil incarnate created the realm and watches over it. Colin Malveaux, however, didn't create your hell. He isn't your fallen angel but is merely a prisoner in a cell with no one in charge."

11

*M*yles didn't say a word for the first two blocks as he headed home with Kendell. "He wasn't necessarily talking about Sanguine."

"The hell he wasn't, and stop reading my mind."

From the moment Brother Aramis had said "fallen angel," Myles knew Kendell would fixate on Sanguine being the logical ruler of her grandmother's hell.

"The story of Satan revolves around him trying to usurp power from God. *Fallen angel* referred to him being banished from heaven. Sanguine doesn't fit either description. She was attempting to fulfill her grandmother's plan, not replace it with one of her own. If anyone should be hell's ruler, it would be Agnes Delarosa."

Kendell held his hand as they walked along Royal Street. The sound of her shoes scraping along the concrete sidewalk made him feel like he was dragging his kid sister home from a fight.

"You and I heard two very different stories from Brother Aramis," she said. "He might be willing to accept some connection between voodoo and the Church, but he wouldn't even say the word *Wicca.*"

Myles had noticed the omission as well. "Have you considered that he might not know that much about Sanguine or her grandmother? From what I could make out, most of the people the Church kept an eye on were residents of New Orleans. Sanguine and her grandmother lived pretty much off the grid out there in the swamp."

"You mean until we came along. When it comes to stories about witches and the Church, Sanguine's distrust might be well-founded. Now that she's been so active with us, the Church has taken notice. She probably doesn't see this life as the refuge it once was."

Myles feared where Kendell's thoughts might be headed. "Look, we're not going to let her move to hell and take up her grandmother's cause or pursue her plan of removing Colin from existence. We'll be her family, and that will give her a reason to stay among the living. But Brother Aramis had a good point. Colin isn't the devil to this version of hell. He's trying to escape. If we can't resurrect Agnes to play the role of hell's ruler, we need to find a way to make Colin accept whatever realm we dump him into."

"A blank slate where he gets to form his own hell?"

Myles wondered how many hells were out there. "No. Brother Aramis also said a devil wants followers. Given a blank dimension, Colin would try to entice—or force—others to join him."

"That's almost what we're facing now, only instead of

moving people into his dimension, he wants to take over ours."

Myles tried fitting the pieces together, but it was as though multiple puzzles had been mixed together. "Not necessarily our reality, just the one he thinks you inhabit."

"What are you thinking?"

He wasn't sure, but talking it out helped. "We can't build a new dimension. The Church won't take our castoff. Left on his own, Colin will blast a hole between his reality and ours, but only to get to you. Ideally, we want him to accept the hell he's in. That would be the simplest answer. We already know we can move voodoo totems from his reality to ours, and Delphine confirmed that we can send a totem back to hell. The real trick is making sure the energy he's building up in the World Trade Center doesn't actually blow a hole between dimensions and continue to pump his evil into our world. We'll need a way to utilize that energy."

Her eyes bore into his like she was pulling the ideas straight from his brain. "If we make mirrors of ourselves so convincing he couldn't tell the difference, and positioned them in his hell, he might think he'd made his way back to our reality. But a virtual hell built on top of his current dimension would need a lot of power to make it run."

He shook his head, trying to see all the specifics. "We've seen his hell. It's only a charade of the real thing. We would need more than just people. Then there's the whole time-standing-still problem. Don't forget, Agnes spent most of her life building just the simplistic version of New Orleans. We're talking about a layout so precise it would fool the man who provided much of the funding that built what we see. Even once we were ready, we'd have to time our additions to when he tried to escape."

"True, but yours is the first idea I've heard that doesn't end up with a tear in the fabric of life and death."

"I wonder what Sanguine will say."

THOUGH SANGUINE HAD LEARNED to find comfort on any flat surface she called home, having spent the better part of two months comatose on Kendell and Myles's couch made crashing on the same cushions a bit awkward. She longed to return to the swamp, but without her grandmother, the old cabin that hung in the trees no longer felt like home. The vision of her grandmother as a young woman and the cabin freshly painted wasn't one she wanted diminished by reality.

Kendell might see her as a sister, but the day was coming when she or Myles would start making subtle comments about Sanguine finding another abode. Where she really wanted to go was back to hell with her wings and ability to see the future, but that wasn't an option, at least not so long as Myles held the only key to her returning.

For a clairvoyant, Sanguine had surprisingly few ideas regarding her future.

When the lovebirds returned from their clandestine meeting with the church elder, Sanguine prepared herself for the eviction. *Better to throw myself out than be tossed on the street.* "I've overstayed my welcome. You two must want your privacy back. I'll find some place to crash."

Kendell looked at her as if she'd lost her mind. "You're family, and you're being ridiculous."

Myles looked less decisive. "We would never kick you out, but I might have an option if you're looking for your own place. The Scratchy Dog has an upstairs that used to be an apartment. Charlie and I use it mostly for storage, but we've got plenty of room for the inventory. Say the word, and the place is yours."

"No charge," Kendell added. "It would be nice to know someone was keeping an eye on the place. I'm sure Charlie could find a job for you if you wanted to make a few bucks."

Sanguine laughed. "Yeah, as a shot girl. Can't you just see me in a skirt so short you could see the curve of my ass, flirting and forcing drinks down the throats of drunk college dudes? I don't think I'd last one night. But I will take you up on the apartment. Honestly, I was a little concerned about where I'd end up."

Kendell sat on the couch and put her arm around Sanguine's shoulders. "I guess we've spent so much time in other realms that we haven't paid a lot of attention to how you'd fair in this one. New Orleans must seem like another dimension to you."

Sanguine couldn't bring herself to tell Kendell how right she was. "How did the meeting with the monsignor go?"

"We have a plan, but it's complicated."

Sanguine listened as attentively as she could manage. When Kendell finally shut her mouth, Sanguine couldn't take it any longer. "You really are out of your mind."

Myles pulled out a pad of paper and started making

some notes. "We realize there are a lot of moving parts, and they'll all need to fit together perfectly."

"You think?" Sanguine wasn't on board, but she managed to resist stomping around the room.

Once Myles started listing the elements of a plan, there was no distracting him. "First, we need to figure out how to make mirror images of every person in New Orleans. Of course, the only real important ones would be those in close proximity to Colin. Anyone a block away probably would just need to look like a mannequin."

Sanguine leaned forward. "He's going to interact with them. Have you thought about that? For example, we can't know the history he has with his secretary. Some things can't be faked. He's going to see right through your plan the minute he talks with someone he knows."

Myles pointed the eraser of the pencil at her. "Good point. Our mirrors will have to reflect the actual people he knows. We should be able to come up with a list pretty easily."

"Then what?" Sanguine asked. "You're just going to download their memories into some voodoo totems? This is never going to work."

Kendell snagged a piece of paper from Myles's pad and started jotting down names. "We don't have to include everyone he's ever met, just those we choose to mirror in his hell. His mother, uncle, secretary, and a handful of others. Everyone else can be out of town. There was a hurricane after all."

Sanguine couldn't believe they were even discussing a

virtual reality. "Fine. So you've got this handful of people. What about you?"

Kendell stopped writing. "Of course I'll have to be mirrored. As will everyone I've worked with in pursuing Colin."

"And if he turns Mirror Kendell into Sexbot Kendell?" She knew it was a cruel question, but Kendell needed to be shocked back to reality.

"Won't happen," Kendell said. "I can put in restrictions."

Myles tapped his pencil against the coffee table. "Then it won't be real enough to fool him. Sanguine's right. For this to work, Colin has to believe he can win you over. We can distract him from business conquests by saying everyone's out of town due to the hurricane, but that's only going to make him double his focus on you."

Kendell started doodling a cartoon of herself. "So Mirror-Kendell becomes Evil-Kendell?" She put horns and a devil tail on the sexy drawing.

"It has to be a possibility," Myles said, "but not an inevitability. However, isn't that kind of what we've done with the seven gates? He has to think he can win or he won't bother playing our game."

Sanguine still didn't see how this was going to work. "You're still not answering my question. How are you going to build these androids?"

Myles returned to his pad. "We need to understand more of what Delphine was talking about. I'm not saying we sacrifice a piece of our souls like ripping our hearts out of our chests, but we should be able to find the equivalent of giving a pint of blood."

"And you're going to sneak in like vampires and take the blood of the chief of police and bank president? Even if Colin's uncle mistrusts his nephew, his mother will never go along with your plan."

"I wasn't saying actually giving blood, just the spiritual equivalent. My point was that Delphine is our resident expert in creating the mirrors. As for the android aspect, though you've proven that spirits can take on physical forms in his hell, we can't rely on your angelic magic."

Kendell drew Sanguine as a beautiful angel next to her devil self-portrait. "Professor Yates is pretty good with mechanisms of a paranormal nature. Though they don't need to be robotic, they will need to be more than holographic."

Sanguine hated when her mind started formulating an argument that helped the other side, but she couldn't help sharing it. "It may not be that complicated. My grandmother's version of hell is a little like a whole-body virtual-reality suit that Colin wears. He can still sense his body getting older, but how he interacts with his environment is kind of a simulation."

Kendell threw her pencil on the table and stared at Sanguine. "So none of this is real? You've let us run around like voodoo chickens with their heads cut off for no reason at all?"

"Of course not. I said her hell was *like* a virtual reality. Clearly, there is a real danger of him breaking through. All I was trying to say is, we don't need hell robots. If you can make the mirror images real enough, we should be able to inject them into my grandmother's program without the need for building physical bodies."

Kendell shook her head as if what Sanguine said made no sense at all. "Fine. Then Professor Yates can build a viewing device in this reality to record people milling about, and we can project that, along with the people-mirrors, into Colin's hell."

Myles returned to his list. "Watch out for step one—it's a doozy. Step two shouldn't be as bad. We can't just plug step one into Colin's hell without some hardware upgrade, so to speak. Though the people might be physical holograms, Professor Yate's projector will need to actually be in hell. With my cane, I can make the trip back through Guinee, but I'm not willing to risk either of you making the trip back to hell. We'll need a go-between."

"Seems like a perfect job for the embassies," Kendell said. "Delphine's Scratch and Sniff, Luther's World Trade Center, Our Lady of Mercy convent—if we can round up enough of them, each might work as a small projection booth. And unlike the bank or police station, those who run the embassies might be willing to help."

Myles scribbled down some notes in the "Step Two" section. "We're getting ahead of ourselves. Without knowing what Professor Yates comes up with, we don't know what he'll need. But for my list, I'll leave the embassies as possible answers. So we have our new reality, and we have our way of projecting it into hell. Now comes the really tricky part. We have to convince Colin that our fake reality is the one he wants to break into."

"I wish I'd kept that golden guitar pick," Kendell said.

"With my connection to the curse isolated in it, he'd probably follow it like a dog chasing a car."

Sanguine couldn't believe she was helping with this madness. "Having it already in his hell, though, makes it easier for us to convince him you're there. That stupid little voodoo pick might be the lynchpin to your whole plan. It contains a piece of your essence—your connection to the Malveaux curse—and it's already in hell. Once your plan of getting him to think he's leaving hell only to end up back where he started is complete, that pick might work as a Kendell beacon to convince him he's in the same world as you."

"It's also a physical object," Myles added. "Professor Yates used to drone on and on about energy left in objects."

Kendell stopped her doodling. "I remember. You pursuing his ideas is what drew us together."

He smiled at her. "Even if Colin did figure out our ruse, he might stay if he thought you were with him. His make-believe will become more enticing than our reality."

"The curse comes full circle." Kendell looked entirely too pleased with herself.

Sanguine almost hated bursting her bubble. "He's going to know the difference between his hell and our reality. The stupid little hunk of gold isn't going to be enough to confuse him. And since it's already in hell, it won't work as the Kendell bait you'll need to convince him to change realms."

"True," Kendell said. "But it does give us an end point for the chase. He'll be back in hell but with a virtual overlay that will make him think he's escaped back to the land of the living. And with the voodoo guitar pick pumping my energy into his world, he'll believe the mirror image of me is the real me. Which I guess brings us to Myles's step three."

He put pencil lead to paper. "He's going to try to escape, and we know, from him giving Kendell his cufflink, that he's using her as his bull's-eye. Which brings us back to Delphine's idea of capturing a part of Kendell, adding it to Baron Malveaux's cufflink, and putting it in a voodoo totem. Then me tossing the totem into his dimension but at a time just after he sets off his escape bomb. Simple."

"Right," Sanguine said. "That's where I step off your crazy train. Kendell is not a rabbit sacrifice used to attract the fox into a snare."

Myles played with the pencil. "We're in complete agreement on that point. As Kendell taught me, sometimes the best way to find an answer is to jump to the next step. This whole plan depends on waiting for Colin to make his move. If we dump our virtual reality into his world too soon, he'll know it's not real. He has to make his escape. Once he's chasing down Kendell to get to our time and space, then we change his reality so when he catches her— or rather the mirror-image of her reflecting off the golden guitar pick in his hell—he thinks he's won."

Sanguine couldn't believe how flimsy the idea sounded. "So your whole plan hinges on waiting for him to do something? What, we're just going to spend all our time staring in our gates to hell, hoping to get a glimpse of him getting ready to leave? Even if I accept every item on your piece of paper, you'll never be able to spring the trap exactly when you need to. And what happens to the essence of Kendell you put into the totem?"

Myles slowly set the pencil onto of the pad of paper. "You're right. I only see one way of making this whole plan work, and it depends on you."

After spending her life with the swamp creatures, she knew when a snare had been tripped, just as she knew the increased adrenaline of being the one trapped. "You want me to return to his hell but to pursue your agenda, not mine. And I assume, from what you've intentionally not said, it will be up to me to save Kendell. Has anyone told you you're a sneaky bastard?"

Kendell put her arms around Sanguine. "He is a sneaky bastard, but his plan does beat the Church's alternative of making you into Colin's Satan. We're putting an awful lot of trust in you to do the right thing, and I'll be relying on you as my protection from Colin while in hell."

$\mathcal{M}$yles found Luther Noire to be far more amenable to his ideas now that Myles had helped with his rescue. He didn't even have to go through Joe Cazenave to enter Luther's building. The cantankerous old goat still smoked his pipe behind his desk like an old-time banker considering loaning money, though Myles suspected that was only because he lacked social skills. Professor Yates sat beside Myles like some overly attentive father ready to cosign the loan. Myles was amazed that both men listened to his plan without butting in with their opinions.

"So what we need is a way to record every action in the French Quarter and some means of projecting all those videos into Colin's hell."

Luther let out a swirl of smoke from his pipe. "You'll need more than that. Every store will need to be stocked, every restaurant will have to prepare food, clubs like your

Scratchy Dog will have to put on performances—basically everything New Orleans is known for will need to be replicated."

"Then there's time itself," Professor Yates added. "The torture of Colin's hell is his lack of time. There's not really any point in proceeding if you can't convince that old swamp witch to change her ways."

The conversation with Sanguine the previous night regarding her grandmother had lasted so late that Myles, Kendell, and Sanguine had all fallen asleep in the living room with the two dogs.

"Once we know we have all the pieces in place, Sanguine will go back to hell. She's going to have a sizable amount of work ahead of her, not least of which is going back in time. She'll have to meet with her grandmother. If the two swamp witches can't come to an agreement, the whole plan will come to a stop. But if they can, we have to be ready."

Luther stroked the bowl of his pipe. "If time moves, Colin will experience the need for sleep and food. He'll consider those biological needs powerful indicators that he's succeeded in returning home."

Myles felt like he was presenting a doctoral dissertation to a review board. "If Professor Yates can develop a way to record people in the Quarter, experiences like eating shouldn't be too hard to replicate. After all, it's not like the menus change all that often. And musical groups have been recorded on both audio and video for generations."

"Polite of you to not say *since we were boys*," said Luther. "I get your point. The whole experience may be beyond the technological abilities of current virtual reality, but we have the advantage of actual places and experiences to build from. What do you expect from me?"

"Colin used this building to project his energy into our paranormal streams when we were creating the seven gates that hold him in hell. I'm hoping to tap into that same power to run our simulations. If we don't, this whole plan will literally blow up in our faces."

Luther leaned forward in apparent interest. "I've been keeping an eye on him as best I can. He has the controls, but he can't stop my gauges from telling me what he's doing. He's kept the bomb from exploding, but barely. If your plan works, we'll have all the power you'll need. Plus, our reality won't depend on him keeping a lid on things. Count me in."

Myles was never sure how far to trust either man, but being men of science, they didn't usually overstate their abilities. He turned in his chair to face Professor Yates. "Now, how about those virtual-reality cameras and projectors?"

"I've got some ideas. I hope you kept your class notes from The Transfer of Human Energy into Inanimate Objects, because we're going to need to put some of that theory into practice."

～

MYLES HELD Kendell's hand as they walked down Esplanade toward Professor Yates's office. "Thanks for coming with me."

"It's like we're back where we started. Do you even remember me in his class? I was such a recluse back then."

He'd had many experiences reading energy and taking trips to the *deep waters*, but the philosophy class meant to investigate such ideas had proved to be mostly a hoax and hadn't been sanctioned by the college.

"You sat in the back row," he said, "wore a black trench coat, and didn't say a word for the entire semester."

"That's not true. I did participate. It's just that no one was listening. You and the others were more interested in disputing everything Professor Yates had to say."

Myles feared that dredging up memories of his distrust of the old man wasn't going to help with their current dilemma. "His philosophy didn't match my reality. I'm not sure which one of us has changed, but I find his ideas more palatable now than I did a few years ago."

"Do you think he can build what we need?"

Myles could remember many discussions with Professor Yates about the atoms of the classroom walls being affected by everything that went on in the room, but none of them were likely to result in a usable gadget. "He's surprised me at times, but even if he could build something, I fear Colin might notice it."

"So we'll make it invisible." She knocked on the glass-and-metal door before Myles could respond to her joke.

"Come on in. I'm just finishing getting set up."

Myles pushed open the door, expecting the one-time receptionist's office to be filled with all manner of semiuseless equipment. To his surprise, the room was empty except for three chairs and a desk. "You haven't gotten started? I thought you'd have something to show us."

With his hair in disarray and his clothes so rumpled they

looked like he'd slept in them, Professor Yates had the air of a mad scientist. "Not this time. We need to delve into the ideas we discussed in class first."

Myles didn't have time to be lectured to again about stuff he already understood. "I've already proven I can read energy left in objects. Hell, that's what started this misadventure."

The professor motioned them to the chairs. "You can only identify events based on strong emotions. What you experience would be comparable to hearing a recording of Thomas Edison yelling into his megaphone and having his voice recorded on a wax cylinder. Playing it back, we can barely make out the words. The level of accuracy we're going to need to fool Colin would be comparable to a symphony recorded in a studio and played back on a high-end digital surround-sound system."

Myles settled back into the chair. "I see your point. Kendell and I have dabbled with fine-tuning my abilities, but I end up getting lost in the overlapping currents of past events. For me, it's like listening to a tape that's been recorded over too many times or a multiexposed picture. At some point, the noise is too much for me to decipher."

"Exactly," the professor said. "But for Colin, we don't need him to experience the past, just the outermost layer of activity."

Myles couldn't quite grasp what the professor had in mind. "We're talking about what I'm able to experience. Even though I've been able to take Kendell on a psychometric trip or two, even I don't know how I do it, only that I can. How does any of this transfer over to Colin?

And if it did, what good would it do for him to read a single object?"

Professor Yates ran his hand over the surface of the metal desk. "Imagine if every man-made object in the Quarter was able to record what's happening here— something we've already discussed—and project those sights, sounds, smells, and tastes into Colin's hell."

Kendell leaned forward and looked at the tabletop as if trying to see the results of Professor Yates's ideas. "That's why you don't have any equipment set up. You don't intend on using any."

"In spite of your lack of participation in class, you always were the brightest student I ever had. As Luther said, we have all the energy we'll ever need from what Colin has built in his hell. We just need to plug the electric guitar into the amplifier, so to speak."

Kendell put her hand on the side of the desk like she was checking to see if a stereo speaker was working. "Now you're talking in a language I understand. We have the instruments—every object in the Quarter—and we have the power. By using the buildings Agnes put in her hell, we even have the speakers, but what constitutes the amplifiers?"

"That's what we need to figure out. With Myles's ability to read energy, he can act as my test subject for fine-tuning the output. We'll need our system to be perfect before going live."

Kendell grabbed Myles's hand the way he did hers when the subject turned to putting her in danger. "I've been on some of his psychometric journeys. The sense of reality is overwhelming. How can we be sure magnifying the experience, even as a test subject, won't result in Myles losing his way back to our reality?"

Myles could already feel his head spinning. "That's kind of the point, though. We want Colin so convinced he's in this reality he doesn't question what he sees."

Kendell bit her lip. The action indicated to Myles she had an idea he probably wasn't going to like. "You might be able to do more than just be Professor Yates's guinea pig." She giggled at her unintended pun. "I didn't mean the voodoo version but the test-subject animal."

Myles was too apprehensive to find the joke funny. "What are you thinking?"

"You and Baron Malveaux were connected for a time. I know it's not an experience you like dwelling on, but you two did share a consciousness. And we still have access to the totem we used to contain him after the exorcism even though it's in his hell. I know he's no longer in the spirit jar, but we might be able to infect his thoughts with the thing."

Myles had devoted himself to keeping Kendell safe, and he knew the protective feeling went both ways. But if she was willing to be used as bait, he had to accept a certain amount of danger as well.

"I'm not sure I see the connection," Myles said.

She lowered her head as if not wanting to continue. "You need to inhabit Colin's spirit jar. You'd only have to be connected to him for a moment for him to gain your psychometric ability. Delphine's explanation of being confined to the totem is like being a genie in a jar. It really wouldn't be that bad."

"But that damn thing is in hell. How do you propose removing my soul and taking it to hell?"

Kendell held his hand tightly. "You'll go with me. We've bonded our spirits enough times in your psychometric travels to know how well we fit together. Sharing a totem would be the same thing, except we'd be connected by voodoo instead of psychometry. You can share my spirit jar while Colin is chasing us. Plus, being in the totem should make it easier for you to pilot it through time and dimensions. You wouldn't have to do it by remote control. I know enough about voodoo that once you've landed us in hell, we can leave the statue, and I can put you into his totem. I know you've never been in favor of even a part of me returning to hell. This is your chance to protect me as well as fulfill our plan for Colin."

Though Myles hated the idea of being once again so intimately connected to evil, the prospect of first being bonded to Kendell gave him courage. "I suppose trying to guide your totem through dimensions without being in the thing would be problematic. The last thing I'd want to happen would be to lose you."

Professor Yates began making some notes. "We already understand how those voodoo fetishes are powered—the wooden sculpture feeds its spirit jar. If I work in Delphine's shop while you two are on your life-and-death journey, I can amp up the power to Myles's body while he's transferring his psychometric ability. Colin would get swept away into the experience."

Too much of the plan left Myles feeling like he was agreeing to open-heart surgery conducted by medical students for a class project. "So Delphine cuts out my soul, and Kendell carries me into hell while I pilot the totem. She then confines me to the container that was once used to isolate the asshole who held me captive, and you turn up the power to my body like I'm strapped to an electric chair. What could possibly go wrong?"

"I'll be right next to you the whole time," Kendell said.

He knew she meant it as a comfort, but having her soul also stuck in the same totem, even if they were bonded together, didn't make him feel any better about the operation.

～

KENDELL WAS AMAZED at how fast the plan came together. A week after their meeting with the secretive member of the Church, she was sitting onstage at the Scratchy Dog with the band, Delphine, Professor Yates, and Myles, comparing notes.

Delphine emptied her canvas bag. Dozens of fabric voodoo dolls that looked like tourist-trap junk littered the stage. Each was attached to a piece of stiff white cardboard. "These are what I intend to use as my mirrors." She picked up a small cloth human figure with buttons for eyes and yarn for its mouth and turned it over to show the writing on the flyer. "No one who calls New Orleans home gives these things a second glance. The fake invitation to a Halloween ball should be enough to get these into the hands of the people Kendell identified as Colin's friends and family. They just need to touch the dolls for me to cast my spell. Since he's not married and doesn't have children, we don't need to worry about him dealing with someone on an intimate level. Hell, Lincoln barely talked to his mother, and that's as close a relationship as I've found. Once he became Colin, he pushed away the last of his few associates."

"Makes sense," Polly said. "He wouldn't want rumors to get around that he'd lost his mind."

Kendell passed out the dolls, one to each person, being careful to handle them by the paper backing. "Since he knows each of us, we'll all need mirrors."

Sanguine stared at her as if she expected an answer to her unasked question.

Kendell nodded. "I will, of course, have more than just a mirror, but it's important that I look and sound like everyone else."

Sanguine rubbed the doll between her hands like a washrag and tossed it back to Delphine. "That wasn't my question, and you know it. You'd better tell everyone what you two have planned."

Kendell was happy to let Myles take point. "We couldn't come up with an alternative to using a piece of Kendell's essence."

The room erupted in objections, but Polly's voice carried above the rest. "Then this whole plan stops right now."

"Hang on," Myles said. "I'm no happier about the situation than you are, but let Delphine explain what she's come up with."

Kendell could tell the band members were just waiting to veto anything Delphine had to say.

"We're not leaving a part of Kendell in Colin's hell,"

Delphine said. "The piece of her we use will be retrievable. Think of it as more of a fancy lure than a worm on a hook. Once we've caught the fish, we can remove the lure. He won't be swallowing the worm."

"I'll just be a cute little spinner." Kendell stood and spun around so her dress lifted from her legs. As she'd feared, her joke fell flat.

Polly got up to address her. "You can't possibly expect to go to hell all by yourself."

The band had already proven their willingness to travel to hell and back for Kendell, but she couldn't let them put themselves in harm's way a second time. "I won't be alone. In order to make Colin truly experience the virtual reality Professor Yates and Luther Noire have invented, he will need Myles's psychometric abilities. That means Myles will literally be traveling with me in spirit. He also needs to be in the totem to pilot us between dimensions. Colin needs to go on a chase to think he's moved beyond hell, even if he ends up right where he started."

Sanguine's hard stare was filled with worry. "And how do you two propose getting out of hell? It's always easier to step into jail than to leave."

Delphine picked up one of Kendell's guitar picks and a cloth doll. "The plan all along has been to maneuver Colin back to the golden guitar pick that holds Kendell's connection to the Malveaux curse." She circled the doll around until it was next to the plastic triangle. "Myles will use his cane like a joystick to fly them through time and dimensions until Colin has followed them back to his hell. To get home, Kendell will use her golden guitar pick stuck on Colin's totem that acts as the seventh gate between life and hell. Since part of her essence will be in hell and most of her spirit will still be with her body in life, she'll be standing on both sides of the gate."

Sanguine kept her arms folded over her chest. "That only holds true so long as Colin doesn't realize the door back to the land of the living is standing wide open. He's going to be pursuing her, so he'll know what she's doing. You're talking about using her as bait, but your plan sounds to me like the scene from *Jaws* when the shark is leaping into the boat."

Kendell held Sanguine's hand. "That's where you come in. I'll be relying on you to make sure the two totems stay in Scratch and Sniff."

Sanguine turned to Myles. "And what about you? Kendell might be able to open the seventh gate for herself, but to use the gates, you'd need to go through each one in order. And at the fifth gate, you'd be stuck on the wrong side. Only the seventh gate leads back to the land of the living."

Myles held up his cane. "Delphine's explanation made it sound like I was playing Kendell on the end of my cane like an angler with a fishing pole jerking a lure. Though none of us want to think of her as live bait, the metaphor works better if you think of me as the hook as well as the pole. Once Kendell is in hell and no longer needs my cane, I can reel my soul back to my body."

"You're really okay with this plan?" Polly asked.

"Nope," Myles said. "But I don't see an alternative. I've been over it a dozen times with Kendell and another dozen with Delphine. From what we've seen of the energy buildup in the World Trade Center, it's inevitable that Colin will make a prison break. Hell isn't strong enough to hold him. If we do nothing, he's going to punch a hole between life and hell. Then we'll have to deal with him as a devil among the living. The only enticement we have to lead him on our merry chase is Kendell."

Sanguine put her hands on her hips. "Just for the record, I really hate step one of this plan."

Kendell leaned toward her. "You're step two, if that makes you feel any better."

Sanguine got up from the stage to address the team. "It doesn't, but at least I have a say in what happens. Before Myles allows his soul to be ripped from his body, he'll escort me through Guinee to hell. Once there, I'll return to my avenging-angel persona. Basically, Kendell will be playing good cop to my bad cop. Colin will pursue the evil minx while running from my heavenly being. Once we've completed our adventure, Myles will have to come back through Guinee to let me out of hell. Though time will still pass differently in life and hell, my being able to travel through time will allow us to coordinate a moment for my escape."

"How will you know when Colin makes a run for it?" Kendell asked.

"First, he'll need to sync up his time frame with what he thinks is ours but is really the voodoo totem with the cufflink and your spirit. To punch a hole through dimensions will involve the release of everything he's got, so I expect a calm before the storm. He'll need to turn off that toy train set he's been playing with. The unsustainable accumulation of energy will send waves through my grandmother's reality. I'll be waiting at Scratch and Sniff for the arrival of your totem. You and Myles should be far enough ahead of Colin that as soon as I see you, I can race to the Scratchy Dog to give the signal to the band, who'll be standing watch at the second gate. They'll signal Professor Yates and Luther Noire to start up our virtual overlay."

Kendell hoped after Sanguine had given the signal she'd leave hell, but no amount of pressure had made her agree to the exit timing. "So once the energy is released, Luther can throw the switch—or whatever he does—and we can gain use of the energy dynamo Colin's developed."

Professor Yates smiled at Sanguine as he took her place in the middle of the room. "I guess that's where I come in." He lifted his bottle of Abita Amber. "Since what we're transferring into Colin's hell is recordings of human energy, I thought the easiest way of differentiating what's current from what's past is to amplify what people are currently feeling. Through Myles's contacts in the bartending world, we've been able to stock every drinking establishment in the Quarter with my turbo alcohol." He took a drink. "It's subtle but has a delayed kick."

Myles distributed open bottles of beer to everyone. "We need your opinion on how it tastes. Not everyone drinks beer, of course, but our alcoholic addition can be used to spike any drink. Because of beer's lower alcohol content, our addition would be more noticeable in a brew than a mixed drink."

Kendell preferred a darker beer, and not just because Abita labeled theirs as Turbo Dog, though the name didn't hurt. "Tastes about the same, but I can definitely notice the higher alcohol content. It'll probably go over big with the college crowd. Do you intend to market it in some way?"

Myles shook his head. "I had Charlie do the legwork. His recommendation was to tell each bartender they would secure a loyal following among their patrons by spiking the drinks. After a shot or two, each one was more than happy to take the free bottles off his hands. Once we secure Colin and establish his reality, we might see how much further we can take the professor's beverage. We'll need to continue the virtual reality for the foreseeable future, so tourists will never consider New Orleans as a place for watered-down beverages. The increased reputation should secure our concoction's place on every bar shelf."

Polly leaned against the wall with her bandmates. "And other than yelling *now* to start the game, what do you want us to do? Wiggle our virtual bottoms to entice Colin to stay in his cage?"

Myles leaned in toward Kendell and whispered, "It's not the worst idea."

She nudged him in the side to keep quiet. "We need you to contact as many of the other gate guardians as you can reach. This whole plan depends on Colin believing he's actually returned to life. If he lets on that he suspects he's being conned, we need to know. You'll be our eyes and ears."

13

*C*olin's time machine atop the World Trade Center required constant tinkering. After living two lifetimes, he knew how time was supposed to flow. Seconds, minutes, and hours might be measurable, but some days and weeks passed faster than others. In spite of what the best clocks had to say on the issue, time was not constant. It was, however, supposed to be predictable.

He checked the brass analog gauge he'd salvaged from the old pumping station. The needle indicated he was a week behind Kendell and the gold cufflink but making up ground faster than intended. "Damn power fluctuations."

He syphoned off more energy to the city's streetlights. Under the influence of his dimension modifier, time moved like a streetcar rumbling down Saint Charles Avenue. For every smooth, consistent hour, there were five minutes where he was sure his machine was about to lurch off the tracks.

The circular room containing every form of analog control he could find reminded him of some Jules Verne classic novel. Computers were useless without the consistent passage of time. He'd never been a fan of steampunk, but his dislike stemmed more from its uselessness than the aesthetic.

He loved looking over his creation. Everything in his control room had a purpose. Some days he saw himself as the mad genius zeroing in on his prey, and others as the monkey pulling levers and turning knobs, hoping for some unseen reward.

The dust-covered piles of paper on the conference table needed attention. Catching up to Kendell was only the beginning. He needed a way to make the jump from his hell back to reality, but the prospect of using his supernatural abilities among the living too easily distracted him from his work. "One thing at a time. Once I link up times, I can focus on building the bridge."

An alarm over the elevator and stairwell indicated an unsafe buildup of energy in one of the vaults. "Really? This is the sixth time this week."

He dialed back his pursuit of Kendell. If he overshot her reality, he might lose his connection to the cufflink. With the gauges all indicating he was keeping time with Kendell but not gaining on her, he headed for the elevator.

Though he had a list of adversaries, on most days he only needed to worry about one: Luther Noire. "I should have killed you when I had the chance. A nice little Halon fire-suppressant cloud, and I wouldn't have to leave my control room every five minutes."

Luther still had his uses of course, and that—not mercy —had been what had prevented Colin from acting on his anger. Losing the totems had been a short-term blow to his plans, but having Luther released from his confinement had proven more challenging. The old fuddy-duddy kept messing with his toys, which nearly created paranormal meltdowns on a regular basis.

Colin fumed as he stepped out of the elevator. The smell of burning electronics stung his nose before the sweltering heat caused sweat to run into his eyes. "Damn it! Seriously? The air conditioners again?" Without a means of cooling the vaults that housed the paranormal objects, their interactions were like angry children on a hot day looking for an excuse to fight. The line between critical mass and meltdown had to be maintained. He followed the smell down a corridor stripped of its sheetrock. The metal beams and exposed wires were a dead giveaway as to the wing's true purpose.

He stopped in front of a solid-metal industrial door that had no place in an office building. Heat radiated off the steel cross members. The oxygen gauge on the wall read "0."

"Okay, either the Halon has kicked in, or the fire has burned out all the air. Either way, you should be cooling down."

He pulled off his long coat and wrapped it around his hand. After investigating numerous near catastrophes, he'd learned to accept whatever he saw inside one of the vaults without applying logic. *Please, no more damn flying monkeys.* The fabric started smoldering from the heat of the half-inch-thick steel lever.

You can't kill me. The mantra had seen him through much worse dangers than an electrical fire. He swung the heavy handle in a sixty-degree arch along the sliding door. Smoke billowed out along all four edges. The acrid fumes made it hard to breathe and worse to see.

The old swamp witch might not let him die, but she'd proven on many occasions that when it came to bodily harm, he was on his own. He threw part of the heavy coat over his head and yanked the door open. The heat enveloped him as though he'd pulled open a blast furnace. Peeking under the heavy fabric, he saw that the comparison extended beyond the temperature. Whatever objects had once been in the room were now a molten mess that covered the floor. A few remaining shelf supports stuck out of the glassy liquid.

Though the vaults had been designed for such eventualities, the safety features weren't designed for multiple failures. "I can't lose another whole floor."

He backed away from the opening and pulled the door shut. The main lever only secured the contents of the room within the building. He turned the red wheel below the handle. A whooshing sound accompanied the rocking of the building. He continued turning the lock until the red light on the door switched to green, indicating the vault had been jettisoned from his reality.

The alarms stopped their incessant screaming. He didn't know where the vaults and their contents had ended up, but all that mattered was that his hell had been saved from the inferno. He reopened the door to reveal dangling wires and metal beams that looked as if they'd been twisted out of place by a hurricane. He could see all the way out to the Mississippi.

"At least nothing came flying at me this time." The relief was short-lived. Luther's collection, though impressive, wasn't unlimited. Too many more meltdowns, and Colin wouldn't be able to wind his magical time machine on the top floor, let alone make the jump from hell to life.

He had only one answer. At least throwing caution to the wind was a risk he understood. "Time to investigate the floor that really makes this place tick."

SANGUINE DESPISED everything about the voodoo realm of Guinee. With its whorehouses used as gates to the afterlife and male-dominated loas of the dead, the purgatory could have doubled as her personal hell. Her biggest irritation, however, was that she had to rely on a dude to provide her safe passage. Myles wasn't such a bad guy, and after he'd provided his soul as a conduit to the life force of the band members, she could no longer lump him in with all the aggressive assholes who thought she should just swoon at their feet. He legitimately cared about women, and not just Kendell. Still, Sanguine would never get used to being led through the streets by the hand like a little girl.

"Aren't we there yet? There has to be a more direct route than weaving through every back alleyway."

"Hush," Myles said. "If anyone sees us, I'll have a devil of a time with the loas. I have no intention of spending eternity in this shithole."

She bristled at being ordered around, but the fact that even he found the realm distasteful validated not only her dislike of Guinee but also her impression of Myles as a good guy.

He slipped into a side doorway and pulled her along after him. "Once you're finished protecting Kendell, get out as fast as you can. I'm not going to be able to make this trip too many more times before the loas catch on that I'm sneaking through their purgatory like a kid cutting through someone's backyard on the way home from school."

He pushed open a door to a cleaning closet. Instead of mops and brooms, Sanguine saw the baron's old office in the bank that doubled as the seventh gate to Guinee.

"As soon as you've figured out how to deal with hell's time continuum, send word through the band's second gate," Myles said. "Kendell will torment my soul in her genie bottle if I can't give her a definite pickup time for your return."

"Yes, boss." She put as much sarcasm into the response as she dared before entering hell.

She literally stumbled out of the bank, realizing as she tripped that the earth was shaking. Earthquakes were a rarity in New Orleans and an impossibility in her grandmother's hell. Her first thought was that Kendell and the team had spent way too much time arguing the merits and finer points of the plan. Colin wasn't the sort to sit back and wait for an adversary. He'd have put the time to good use.

She needed to find him and discover what fresh nightmare he'd concocted. Another quake made her again lose her balance. None of their plans would be worth a damn if hell was about to crumble to the ground. She spread her wings and took off toward the swamp like an angel out of hell.

Her grandmother might have bent time to assist with the forming of the seven gates, but she wouldn't be at her granddaughter's beck and call. Sanguine beat her wings hard and fast. In spite of the dangers, being able to fly again exhilarated her more than the best sex. Her back ached from using muscles she hadn't had five minutes earlier. Her previous flights had been as a spirit's imaginings. This time, the wings were more than just a dream. *If this paranormal skill is back, so too must be my insect sight.*

She aimed toward the open air above Lake Pontchartrain and closed her eyes. She saw the causeway up ahead in her future vision before she opened her eyes. But her destination didn't lie forward in time. She looked to the horizon and swung her attention to the past.

As nothing more than spirit, the experience of flying backward through time had been disorienting, but with her body along for the ride, Sanguine felt positively nauseated. She forced the jambalaya she'd had for lunch farther down her esophagus and let the confusing images flow by her. Fortunately, the lake seldom changed.

Once nights started preceding days in a kaleidoscope of weather events, she lost track of how far back in time she'd traveled. She stopped beating her wings and spread them out to glide over the swamp on a warm summer's day. From the lack of invasive water hyacinth that usually clogged the waterways, she knew she'd gone beyond her lifetime. Before sailing out to her grandmother's cabin, Sanguine took a leisurely glide along the river. Plants were growing so fast she checked her eyesight to make sure she wasn't traveling in an accelerated version of time. She dove among the young cypress grove. This was the beginning of her grandmother's creation—back when it was little more than developing vegetation.

She spread her wings back to their full span and gave them two hard thrusts toward the sun-drenched island. Time might be bendable, but her emotions nagged at her that there was work to do and she needed to get on with it.

The new grass felt good under her bare feet as she lighted on the edge of her grandmother's outcropping of land. A child's laughter made her scurry for the pine forest. *Mom?* Thoughts, questions, and emotions demanded attention, but her mission wasn't to investigate her personal history. *If that is my mother, then Grandma will be alone in the cabin.*

She steeled herself for the strange meeting. The old woman she knew was seldom surprised by anything, but having her granddaughter show up from the future with angel wings exceeded any odd event Sanguine could recall.

The lightly forested section of the island extended from the water's edge to a vegetable garden next to the cabin. Sanguine snuck as close as possible to the open window of the living room at the front of the house. "Agnes Delarosa, are you in there?"

A woman bolted out the front door, wielding a shotgun. Sanguine barely had time to hide beside the house. "Who's there? Show yourself. Don't make me conjure a gator."

"Easy, Grandma." Sanguine never could hide from the woman. She tried to keep her wings tightly gathered behind her as she stepped around the corner of the cabin. "I know this won't make any sense, but I am your granddaughter. I'm from the future."

Agnes heaved the long barrel of the gun over her shoulder. "Come inside before Julia sees you. Last thing that child needs right now is to hear one day she's going to be a mother to an angel."

Though the woman's casual acceptance shouldn't have come as a surprise, Sanguine was just a little disappointed her wings hadn't elicited more of a comment. "I've come to talk about this realm you're building. There's a structural problem."

The woman's laugh reminded Sanguine of the old woman she'd known. "Only one? Watch those wings. If Julia sees a long white feather, I'll never hear the end of questions regarding what magical bird I designed as her personal form of transportation."

Again, Sanguine wanted to ask about her long-lost mother. The questions made her eyes water. "There's a power surge in my time. It's not unexpected. In fact, we intend to use it to run an app on top of what you've built."

"What the hell is an app?"

Sanguine struggled with what words to use. "It's an addition, like a layer of reality we're using to enhance what you will end up creating."

"It's confusing talking across times, isn't it? What do you need from me?"

The personal demands struggled to be expressed, but

Sanguine maintained control of her emotions. "I need you to build in a way for me to access control of your realm. And the underlying structure needs to be stronger. We're having earthquakes."

Agnes set the shotgun behind the door. "So Baron Malveaux figured out how to control my world? Natural disasters work as my alarms."

"It's a little more complicated than that. Our prisoner is only *mostly* the baron."

Agnes sat in the chair she would use as her seat of authority for the next fifty years. "Explain."

Sanguine struggled with how much detail would be needed to fix the energy problem without unduly affecting the future. "A powerful businessman, a descendent of Baron Malveaux, will merge his spirit with the old baron. He had to be stopped. I didn't have a choice."

"Easy, child. You won't be hearing judgment from me. As you've flown out here, I assume you will grow up in this cabin. What shall I teach you?"

Even with her multitime sight, Sanguine knew her grandmother understood the river of time better than she ever would. "My best subjects were plants and animals. I went to Tulane as a biology student." She spread her arms and wings. "Animals understand my words in life, but here in your world, they obey my every thought."

Agnes put the tips of her fingers together in front of her face, a stance Sanguine remembered as her grandmother's way of driving some piece of information into her memory. "I will leave the tools to modify this realm with the animals in my creation. Now that I know it's you who will inherit this dimension, and that it will be needed, I can gear it to your use. Honestly, it's a relief to hear that the baron doesn't make his move sooner. Julia is too sweet a child to do what's needed."

Her grandmother had raised Sanguine to be tough and self-sufficient—both physically and emotionally. Never before had she considered that the old woman might have been trying to correct the mistakes she'd made raising Julia. Confronting the devil wasn't a task for the weak. "I have to go before I mess up my personal future."

Before she could leave, her grandmother got up and took Sanguine's hands. "If you're here, I must be dead in your time, so there will be no harm in telling you that I love and trust you and I always will. Do what you must with my creation. You have my blessing."

Sanguine flew back out to Lake Pontchartrain to consider her options. Thinking about the birds who'd shown her how to fly and the dragonflies who'd taught her about seeing the past and future, she realized that some of the animals her grandmother had mentioned had already found her.

Though the swamp was her home, she did some of her best thinking while staring at the open expanse of the lake. She needed to return to her future, but moving ahead in time proved more challenging than making her way back along the well-known path of history. Sitting on a piling at the end of the long dock separated her from the land. The feeling of isolation matched her sense of time. She hadn't exactly followed the path back to the future she'd taken to see her grandmother. Just stopping at the dock branched her off from the life she knew.

Her insect view of the future only extended a few moments, but those images changed slightly, depending on which way she looked. Growing up, she'd often been told that all futures were possible. Never before had she been so afraid of that truth. *I have to get back to where I started.*

Why? The question was her rebellious side hoping to return to the plan of extinguishing Colin Malveaux from existence. However, the thought of leaving Kendell stranded in hell forced Sanguine to look across the lake for the path through time that led back to her friend. Like her dragonfly mentors, she saw multiple futures as not simply possible. Each branch off of her destiny was every bit as real as the people from the other dimensions she'd met.

She tried to shake the confusing possibilities from her mind. As she stood on the dock, some version of her might fly off to erase Colin, Lincoln, and Baron Malveaux from history. Another Sanguine would fly to the future but as the guardian of hell intent on turning Colin's existence into the torture he deserved. Then there was the Sanguine who loved her friend. Even if she pursued one of the directions she'd envisioned as a means of stopping Colin from ever coming into being, the path that led to Kendell standing in hell with the devil in hot pursuit wouldn't cease to exist.

She leapt into the air and focused her attention on the woman she knew. Kendell needed Sanguine's help, and the only way to find her way back was to follow through on Kendell's plan.

~

KENDELL HAD mixed emotions about Myles putting his soul at risk for her. On the one hand, she hated having to put him in danger, again. His possession by Baron Malveaux had been partly her fault, and she'd never forgive herself. Having to lock souls with who the baron had become had to be a fate worse than death. Though no one could come up with a better answer for how to control Colin, she felt like she was asking the impossible of her partner.

But he wasn't going alone. He'd accepted her help before. She never had any use for the alpha male who didn't know how to let a woman come to the rescue from time to time, and Myles had proven to be far more of a life partner than a dominating boyfriend. He'd taken her on his psychometric outings, and it was only fair for him to now trust her completely with his soul on her voodoo adventure.

She held his hand as they sat in front of Delphine's worktable. "You're stronger than you think you are."

He sat up a little straighter. "The funny thing is, I'm not all that afraid of being stuck with Colin. Baron Malveaux saw me as some snot-nosed kid. He despised me and didn't bother hiding his contempt." Myles kicked his cane, which was leaning against the table. "But this stick wasn't meant for him. It was meant for me. I'm kind of looking forward to bashing him over the head with it."

She tried not to laugh. "Don't get crazy. You're just supposed to sneak in and help him detect the human energy that infects all man-made objects. This isn't a pissing match."

"Maybe not, but it does give a new meaning to 'giving him a piece of my mind.'"

She smiled at his outward desire to protect her. "Don't forget, you're partially doing this to keep me safe. Provoking Colin might not be the best way to do that."

He took his cane and held it between his legs like a joystick. "And the other part is to fly us to hell. That's what really worries me. I've been to Guinee, but this will be my first time traveling between multiple dimensions. Each time I move the cane, we'll be banking through time. Though I know where and when Colin is located, finding him in the interdimensional soup will be a challenge."

"Don't worry. I'll be your navigator."

Delphine finally arrived, carrying her assortment of candles and incense. "I assume Kendell explained what you're in for? This isn't going to be pleasant for any of us."

Myles finally let go of Kendell's hand. "When is anything we do ever enjoyable?"

Professor Yates was next to enter the crowded room. Kendell's fear for Myles increased as the old man wired him up to the array of machinery. "Most of this equipment is so that I can keep an eye on how you're doing physically, so if things get out of hand while you're working on Colin, don't try to hold in your reactions. If you find you have control over your body, clinch your fist, and I'll dial up the power. Open your hand, and I'll reduce the flow."

Myles nodded and took a deep breath. "Let's just get on with it."

Kendell let herself give way to the smells and spells that Delphine used to prod her soul. Myles proved far braver at accepting the voodoo intrusions than she would have guessed. It wasn't long before they were sharing their souls in the voodoo totem. Though only a part of her was in the genie bottle, with Myles fully in the spiritual plane, Kendell found it hard to focus on anything else.

Mentally, Myles pushed his cane forward. The world around Kendell exploded into a whirlwind of images. As a child, she'd dreaded the yearly viewing of *The Wizard of Oz*. Like Dorothy being sucked into the tornado, Kendell lost track of all that she held dear, with the exception of Myles. She kept her eyes open for the devil pedaling his bicycle in pursuit of her through the whirlwind.

In Colin's history with Luther Noire, the secretive guardian of paranormal artifacts had been careful to dodge any specifics about what lay within his vaults. After locking Luther in his office, Colin's first order of business had been to take a thorough inventory of everything he possessed. He'd hoped to find the equivalent of a paranormal brick that he could throw to break the barrier between life and hell. Though he hadn't found what he sought, he did discover that the power to control each vault first ran through the twenty-third floor.

In a jail, the most secure area housed the most dangerous inmates. As the twenty-third was the least accessible floor in the World Trade Center, it had to be where Luther kept the most powerful objects. Even when Colin had command of the elevators, he'd never managed to stop on the concealed floor. He'd tried the stairs, but frustratingly, the door labeled "23" opened to Luther's offices and not to the secured vaults.

The time has come for me to take charge, old man. Colin spread his coat and glided down the building, counting the floors during his descent. With a rap from his iron walking cane, he smashed a window that was supposed to be unbreakable. *I am the devil, and this is my hell. No part of it is forbidden to me.*

Once inside, he walked along the hallway and checked each of the vaults for stability. From the rusted doors and antique gauges, he knew the vaults predated the building.

His investigation wasn't purely driven by curiosity. After figuring out that time wasn't constant, he knew there had to be paranormal objects that affected that force of nature. His machine on the top floor proved such mechanisms were possible. What he'd created, however, was a rocket without a guidance system. He had used his pocket watch with the attached cufflink like a compass while blasting his time engine, but such crude attempts weren't getting him closer to Kendell and too often resulted in meltdowns. He needed something more refined, and he didn't have the patience or skill to design it himself. *Time is the dimension you used to cool your vaults. It has to be.*

The main power line ran into a vault that looked like every other rusted door along the hallway. It opened with a protest of squealing metal. *This is it. All or nothing.* The room was lined with metal storage shelves filled with wooden boxes. Wires ran from the ceiling to each row. By tracing the leads, he found the main junction box. Unlike all of the previous vaults he'd investigated, this one had clocks—both digital and analog—attached to each breaker that led out to the shelves. An old-fashioned white-faced school clock dictated the time to the hodge-podge of timepieces inside the junction box. The second hand moved forward, but the minutes were going in reverse.

He pulled out his pocket watch and the attached cufflink from his waistcoat. Compared to building his control room upstairs, attaching the wires from the main clock to his watch was simple. With the flip of a single lever up in his control room, he could transfer command of the vault from the school clock to his pocket watch.

He felt naked as he left the vault. His jury-rigged piece of jewelry was his only connection to Kendell and reality. If switching how the artifacts dealt with time—and throwing full power to the twenty-third floor—resulted in another meltdown, he'd become a castaway adrift in the middle of time's ocean. If his plan worked, however, not only would he sync up to reality's time, but he might also punch his way from hell back to life.

He just needed the nerve to throw the switch.

Colin stepped out the window and twirled in his long coat to return to the top floor, but when he arrived, he found he wasn't alone. "I thought I banished you from hell, little bug."

Sanguine sat on the circular roof like a sculpted angel on the gable of a church. "This hell doesn't belong to you, so you have no authority to claim or banish anyone. This is my realm now, and I'm here to make sure you realize this hell is your incarceration, not your playroom. We can start by getting rid of that flying coat of yours." She snapped her fingers. A murder of crows descended from the sky and ripped his long coat from his shoulders.

"You're not the only one with little pets." He too snapped his fingers, but his usually faithful bats had abandoned him.

"Guess I should have mentioned my first act was to reconcile with hell's creatures, including your little winged rats."

He'd been outmaneuvered. Being alone in hell had made him complacent, but he still had control of the World Trade Center. Sanguine might fancy herself as some kind of avenging angel, but that didn't give her any power over his machinery.

"So what's your plan? You just going to hover over me and make sure I'm suffering? You don't have that kind of a sadistic nature. You'll get bored within a week."

"My grandmother believed letting you discover your hidden talents was useful in that she could take them away whenever she chose. She thought having something to do would distract you from trying to escape, but you and I know that hasn't been the case. Under my rule, you won't be discovering any supernatural abilities. You'll just be a sad little man condemned to a lonely life."

He marveled at her ability to read his darkest fear. "And what about you? As the jailor, are you going to accept the same fate?"

She stretched out her wings. "I never really cared for more than a handful of people. Though I'll miss them, I'll find enough to keep me occupied with my grandmother's animals."

"So you and I are just going to do battle for eternity? Me forever trying to get you to change your mind about letting me leave, and you tormenting me? Still sounds awfully boring, or was that your intention?"

She hopped down from the roof as easily as she would off a barstool. "Nope. I know you're messing with time, obviously. I'm going to let you keep playing with it. Just realize once time exists as you remember, so does your inevitable death. And backing up the clock doesn't take years off your age. I know. I checked."

He spread his arms so she could see how he'd already aged. "Me getting older doesn't seem to be a function of your grandmother's stoppage of the clocks."

She sighed as though he'd said something stupid. "You're getting older because you expect to get older. But just like those clothes, if you try hard enough, you can mend the lines around your eyes and darken your gray hairs back to black. I would guess you probably already knew that. With time moving forward, the effects will be real and not just theater makeup. You will die of either old age or suicide."

He leaned against the railing. "So if I fell, you'd let me die? You're not like your grandmother. Why not just kill me yourself?"

"I made a promise—a couple of them actually—to let you live. But no one said I had to keep you alive."

Though she had a snarky attitude that reminded him of a teenager who thought she had all the answers, she wasn't bad company, especially considering how long he'd gone between conversations. "You're not concerned my spirit will infect all of humanity with my greed and lust for power? I seem to recall your grandmother setting this little jail cell up for me specifically so my soul wouldn't return to the human continuum. She believed I was the manifestation of everything that was wrong about humanity."

"Oh, I agree with everything she taught me. Your death isn't the end of my adventure—it's more like the beginning. Once you're gone, I intend to travel back through time and erase every one of your deeds all the way back to when Archibald Malveaux was a little boy. Then, as he ages, he'll find life isn't quite as easy as he'd imagined."

Her plan had a simplicity to it that he admired. Having his accomplishments systematically removed from history only to have him start over again as the perpetual pauper made him quiver inside. Fear wasn't an emotion he embraced. With two hundred years of successes, in both life and death, he had developed the confidence to face any challenge with conviction. Having the ability to remove the basis of that iron will, however—now, that was true power.

"Instead of a guardian angel, you'll be a demonic presence tripping me up at every turn. What's to stop me from killing you first?"

She tilted her head as if she'd never considered the idea. "We both have friends in the afterlife. I suspect mine would allow me to continue my mission."

"And if I find a way to escape?"

"You won't."

Apparently, she shared her grandmother's fundamental failing.

"You're overly confident," he said.

She shrugged off the dig. "We'll have plenty of time to

find out." Without waiting for his rejoinder, she ran to the edge of the building and jumped into the air. Her long white wings carried her high into the sky.

"I'm going to miss flying." Though he still considered Kendell a worthier intellectual adversary, he couldn't deny that Sanguine had found ways of cut him deeply.

~

Sanguine flew around the outskirts of the Quarter until she was certain Colin had returned to his science experiment. Once she saw the streetlights flicker, she landed on the roof of Saint Louis Cathedral. A man who'd amassed so much power would never bow down to a young woman. *I'll just bet you're futzing with those knobs and levers like a little boy right now. You just go ahead. I'll be right here, watching and waiting.*

The sun and moon streaked across the sky like dogs chasing each other around the living room. The fact that time no longer moved slowly and deliberately was her first indication of Colin's panic. She only had to wait until the days resumed their normal progression and he shut down his streetcars.

Hunger turned her stomach into a knot of pain. Her eyes stung from lack of sleep. As a spirit, she hadn't endured the physical reactions to Colin's time distortions, but now that she had her body with her, the effects were intolerable. She glided off the sharply angled roof to the cobblestone-paved promenade. *He must be getting close.*

The sooner Kendell's totem showed up in Delphine's

shop, the sooner Sanguine could rescue her friend's spirit and return to life, where she could get some rest. Though the walk was only a handful of blocks, her legs ached so badly from exhaustion that she considered spreading her wings. But she resisted the temptation to fly, figuring that stumbling would be less jarring than falling from the sky. She took a deep breath, hoping the oxygen would rejuvenate her muscles. Her one consolation was that if she was this beat, Colin had to be in worse shape. The distraction would dull him to the changes in his world while the rest of the team powered up their virtual-reality addition to hell.

Sanguine pushed open the door to Scratch and Sniff. Scents of perfume wafted out of the vacant space. She mentally ran through her list of chores again. *First, drive Colin into action. Second, make sure Kendell and Myles arrive in hell, then notify the band. Finally, protect Kendell at all costs.*

She leaned against the wall and watched Kendell and Myles materialize from the voodoo totem. Kendell put one hand on Myles's shoulder and the other on the golden guitar pick atop the second totem. They shared a kiss, and he was gone.

Sanguine knew there wasn't time for pleasantries. "We have to notify the band. There isn't a moment to lose."

Kendell didn't turn from the totem. "You go. I'm staying here until Myles is safely out of this thing. I'm his only hope for rescue."

~

LIKE MOST OF his college friends, Myles had sampled enough mind-altering drugs to know the hallucinogens were more of a distraction to life than an answer. Those experiences paled in comparison to navigating a voodoo totem through interdimensional time and space. The displays of friends being transformed into members of every socioeconomic class he could imagine left him wondering who these people were. He'd thought he knew them. *Polly as a CPA? Scraper as an aid worker in Africa? And what the hell, Charlie? I thought you would always be straight, dude.* He was only spared from seeing Kendell undergo the transformations as she huddled in the totem with him.

But even that psychotic whirlwind into hell was favorable to being stuck in Baron Malveaux's old totem. As opposed to the comfortable, though somewhat cramped, totem Delphine had set up for him and Kendell, the baron's old prison cell reeked of tar and rotting flesh. Ghostly images of the women the baron had enslaved, impregnated, prostituted, and finally held against their will in Guinee floated out of the black goo that covered the walls. Their screams of anguish made it hard for Myles to think. *I'll bet that bastard didn't even notice.*

Myles felt along the cave-like hellhole for some hatch to Colin's soul. He pulled his hand away from the wall. Black slime stuck to his finger and burned his skin. He watched in horror as the thick acid dissolved his flesh down to the bones. The reflex of balling his hand into a fist restored the flesh, though the pain remained. *Agnes Delarosa had nothing on Marie Laveau when it came to designing hells. Good thing Sanguine hasn't seen this place.*

He probed the wall with his cane, hoping the acid wouldn't destroy the loa's gift. Green sparks emanated from the handle and filled the room with a blinding light that made him squeeze his eyes shut. *Sure would have been nice if this thing had come with a user's manual.*

When he opened his eyes, he was no longer in Baron Malveaux's version of hell. He stood in the middle of a dark, hardwood-paneled room. African, Haitian, and voodoo symbols were carved into the walls.

A black woman wearing a flowing kente-cloth dress and head scarf sat on a throne of gold. "Welcome, Myles."

"You know me?"

Her eyes sparkled like sapphires. "I've been waiting for you. Sorry for the mix-up about your cane. My bad."

"You're Marie Laveau?"

"That I am. Unlike some dimensional architects, I keep an eye on what I've created."

"And you know why I'm here?"

She pointed at the cane. "You're here to fulfill that staff's destiny. By instilling empathy in Colin Malveaux, you will give him the ability to see the error of his ways."

Myles could feel the stone under the silver skull handle of the cane growing warm in his hand. "Um, actually I'm here to give Colin my psychometric skills so he'll be able to see the virtual-reality overlay we're creating for his hell."

"Same thing. You're able to read energy people have left behind because you don't just understand people—you connect with them at a basic soul-wide level. You experience our universal connection. Archibald, Lincoln, and Colin did all they could to separate themselves from people. Only someone completely devoid of empathy could treat others as if they're nothing more than his personal playthings."

In spite of his paranormal ability—which he'd been told all his life was mere daydreaming and foolishness—Myles never considered himself all that special. "Why me?"

She shrugged. "I suppose you could ask that question about anyone's life. Why did I become who I was and Archibald become Baron Malveaux?"

"But you worked at becoming the voodoo queen, and Baron Malveaux didn't sit back and let evil come to him."

Marie stared at Myles as if waiting for the answer to form in his mind.

"It's not the same for me," he continued. "I was never trying to be anyone."

"Weren't you? Do you really believe I was all about the title? My passion was understanding what lay beneath the surface layer of life. Tell me that same curiosity didn't drive you to where you're currently standing."

He suspected the argument was one of those that could take a lifetime to work out. "I'm sorry I asked. What am I supposed to do?"

"The key is the women you saw in his totem."

Myles knew enough of the baron's past to figure out the poor souls had once lived elegant lives and had husbands and children before being turned into sex slaves by the baron's greed and perversion. "I thought they'd all moved on to the *deep waters*. Please don't tell me you've kept those lost souls prisoners just to torment Baron Malveaux."

"Don't worry. The work you and Kendell did saved them

from the baron's control. What you saw weren't souls. They were the baron's version of guilt. He couldn't internalize what he'd done, so he created those images like a cave painter drawing on the walls. They don't exist, but they are real to him."

"So if I convince them they have value and that they aren't just toys for him to use, that will create some connection in him for the people he abused? And in so doing, he'll gain a modicum of empathy, which will allow him the psychometric vision needed to see what we're projecting?" Myles hadn't realized his task was going to be so hard.

"No one said your mission in life would be easy."

14

*M*yles came to on the couch in the apartment he shared with Kendell. Doughnut Hole was licking his face with such determination he thought the puppy must have been trying to revive him with dog slobber. "It's okay, boy. I made it home."

On the chair, Kendell held Cheesecake, who was whimpering something awful. "Finally. I was starting to fear our new couch came with a sleeping spell attached."

He couldn't remember Cheesecake ever putting up such a racket. "What's with your girl?"

"She hasn't stopped acting like I'm sick since you took that piece of my soul to hell. Maybe now that she sees you're awake, she'll believe me that everything is going to be okay."

He struggled to remember where he was supposed to be. "What happened in Delphine's office? I thought my body was wired up to Professor Yates's contraption."

She set Cheesecake on the ottoman and sat at Myles's side. "It was. Once we knew you'd succeeded with Colin, we brought you back here so you could rest in comfort."

His head buzzed from too many dimensions. "This is the worst hangover ever. How long have I been out?"

Her hand on his forehead reminded him of his mother's loving touch when he'd been sick as a child. "Eleven hours and twenty-three minutes, give or take thirty seconds."

He laughed, which made his head pound harder. "You timed me?"

"Me and the dogs have been pretty worried. Doughnut Hole hasn't left your side since Professor Yates and Charlie carried you home."

He struggled to sit up. "How are you? And where are we with the hell modification?"

As his eyes began to focus, he noticed why Cheesecake had been so worried. The dark circles under Kendell's eyes made her look as though she hadn't slept in days.

"I'm not whole yet. The part of me in hell still has work to do, but don't worry—I'm with Sanguine. Professor Yates and Luther were able to start up their virtual-hell projection. So far, everything seems to be working. Colin was knocked out from his time-travel adventure, so we had to wait for him to come to in order to find out if everything was working. From the way he interacted with our voodoo-doll people, we could tell you'd succeeded in making him see what we wanted him to see."

Myles held his head and tried to remember everything that had happened in the spirit realm. "I had the weirdest conversation with Marie Laveau. Something about Colin's lack of empathy being the root of his problem and me having to make him understand people. My memories are pretty jumbled after that. Any idea how I made it home?"

"The totem reemerged on Delphine's table." Her voice quivered, though he couldn't tell if it was from exhaustion or remembered fear. "It took both of us to get you out."

His time in Baron Malveaux's totem had been fuzzy, and he had no memories at all of piloting his way home. "I'd have to guess Marie Laveau spirited me home. Guess I'll have to reconsider my disbelief in all those sea stories about ghosts captaining vessels home after the sailor was knocked out in a storm."

"However you did it, I'm just glad you're home."

His thoughts were beginning to clear. "Wait. Why are you and Sanguine still in hell?"

She moved her hand from his head to his side. "I know what I'm doing, both here in life and there in hell. Right now, alternate me is sitting with Sanguine in the Scratchy Dog while she gets a few hours of sleep onstage. We wanted to be somewhere we could be watched from one of the gates. Colin progressed time too fast for her to adjust. We suspect the same was true for him. With him knocked out, Professor Yates and Luther had time to fine-tune the projection."

"What about the you that's sitting here with me?"

"I'm a little disoriented, but we have to make sure Colin completely believes it's me he's seeing, or else he'll never buy into our ruse."

"You're only spirit in hell, so how are you going to make

this scheme work?" Myles said, trying not to sound like the judgmental boyfriend.

"Delphine created a voodoo doll for me along with everyone else. In his realm, those walking, talking, living projections are completely solid. I inhabit that doll. He'll never notice anything different about me from any other person."

"And the archangel Sanguine? With those wings and eyes, she's not going to pass unnoticed."

"She's one of the reasons I had to stay," Kendell said. "I'm still concerned she sees this virtual reality as a way of lulling Colin into a sense of security then continuing with her ultimate plan of wiping him from history."

Myles thought Sanguine's plan was more based on emotion than logic, but her idea had its merits. "I don't want to see her fly off into the past never to be seen again either. I know that's your biggest worry."

Kendell shook her head. "In some alternate reality, I'm sure that's exactly what she does. I'm worried that what she can't see is that erasing his deeds only creates another dimension. Nothing she does can change the past as we know it. *Our* reality remains the same. All she would accomplish is leaving us to deal with Colin on our own."

Imagining all the different versions of life renewed Myles's dimensional hangover. "Have you tried explaining that to her?"

"She's sleeping. Trust me, getting that message through her thick skull is my first objective. Once she understands that her plan won't make any difference, and we're sure Colin is buying into his new reality, I'll work with you to reunite my spirit and get both me and Sanguine out of hell once and for all."

~

FOR ALL OF her assurances to Myles, Kendell knew convincing Colin he had returned to life wasn't going to be easy. As someone who'd spent so much time alone in hell, he would find ways of testing everyone and everything to make sure he wasn't dreaming. She and Sanguine were the only real people in the dimension who could tell if the plan had been effective, and time was running out before Colin started poking around his new playroom.

But Sanguine was also going to be a challenge. The young swamp witch had a drive to honor her grandmother that rivaled Delphine's obsession with Marie Laveau, and that meant Colin had to suffer in the hell the old swamp witch had created. Kendell hoped Sanguine would listen to logic if it were presented in a loving manner. Colin needed to believe this was a continuation of the life he remembered if they stood any chance of keeping him contained.

The real problem, however, was Kendell herself, or rather the sliver of herself that was playing in hell like a witch dancing with naked abandon around a bonfire.

As Kendell strapped on her electric guitar for the nightly gig at the Scratchy Dog, she felt her alternate self doing the same but filled with more excited anticipation. Kendell looked over at Myles, who was tending bar with Charlie. The normalcy of the scene gave her comfort.

The sliver of her in hell, however, was eyeing Colin

Malveaux, who had just stepped into the club. To avoid the distraction, she turned to her fellow bandmates who, though mirroring the actions of the real people they represented, had about as much depth as cardboard cutouts.

The two versions of herself doing almost identical actions quickly became so disorienting that Kendell feared she would inadvertently give away the deception. *Here in life, I'm Kendell. There in hell, I'm Endall. The name is subtle enough that if I slip up I can explain it away by too much alcohol. Plus, I like the play on words.* She smiled at her brilliance, though she knew most of the self-congratulations came from Endall.

Kendell turned to Polly. "Let's play something loud. My fingers are aching to wail away at these strings." She suspected the desire to stand out musically came from her alter ego's longing to shove her music down Colin's throat.

As the night wore on, Kendell lost track of what songs they'd played. Endall was consumed with taking center stage even though Kendell kept to her spot behind Polly. Once she finally pried her fingers off the neck of the guitar, she had trouble straightening them out.

"That was pretty intense playing, sister." Polly sounded like she'd been ridden hard, and Kendell knew it was her hard-driving beat that had been doing the riding.

"Good thing we've got tomorrow off. At least the tips should be impressive."

Polly helped round up the equipment. "I kind of thought with you not being at full strength the rest of us might catch a break. Mind telling me where that energy came from?"

Though she'd played with vigor, Kendell hadn't

considered how much of the night had been directed by Endall. "Guess I plugged into some hellish energy."

"Just don't let it become another addiction."

⌇

ENDALL DESPERATELY WANTED to keep playing. She'd have gone all night had the rest of the band not been such stiffs. Reluctantly, she put her black guitar back in its case. Looking back up, she saw Colin approach the stage.

"I wasn't sure what to expect when you saw me. I hope that intensity wasn't your way of directing your anger at me."

Kendell was demanding Endall play her part. Colin supposedly had escaped hell, and she was supposed to be surprised and pissed, not excited. "So what if you broke out? We played our cards, and you played yours. Looks like you won again." She hoped her annoyance would cover her lack of surprise.

"Can we go somewhere private to talk?"

From the back of her mind, Endall felt Kendell sigh in relief. Colin believed they weren't alone, which meant he was accepting all the moving mannequins as real people. "There's an old speakeasy out back. Give me a minute to clean up. If you feel like buying a girl a drink, I could use an Abita Turbo Dog."

"Whatever my lady desires."

She watched the exchange between Colin and cardboard-cutout Myles with mild curiosity. Her voodoo-doll boyfriend did such a good rendition of the pissed-off lover she worried the two men might end up duking it out in the street. Cardboard Charlie intervened before things got physical. *Not bad for a first interaction. Even I couldn't tell Myles was a fake.*

Talking to herself was taking on a whole new meaning. *Just don't get carried away by Colin's charms. Remember, he's supposed to have broken out of the prison made up by me and Sanguine. If that had happened, I'd be a little damaged.*

Yes, Mom. But Endall knew the warning was justified. She had control over Colin and his hell. If the devil discovered he was being played, she'd have to call in Sanguine for reinforcement, and everyone had done too much work to have to start all over again. Before getting offstage, she gave Polly a hug just to see how it would feel.

"You did good tonight," Polly said. "I'm just glad we don't have to play with that intensity every night."

"Afraid you can't keep up?" Endall couldn't resist the snarky little rejoinder.

"Just watch yourself. Remember, you're not at full strength."

Endall looked deep into the bandleader's eyes and saw the telltale sparkle of Sanguine's reflective insect irises. "Nice to know I'm not alone."

"Want me to tag along for your discussion with Colin?"

As Polly, Sanguine might pass as nothing more than a chaperone, but for Colin to fully trust Endall, she needed to take him on alone. "I've got this."

"Just don't fuck it up."

Endall stepped off the stage and headed out the back door of the club.

Colin sat at the table often used by Myles to talk to the loas of the dead. "You seem surprisingly unconcerned at seeing me, or should I expect some interdimensional guardian force to sweep me back to my hell?"

She sat at the table and enjoyed the first sip of the dark beer. The thick, chocolaty head tickled her nose. *Another successful test—this beer tastes exactly as I remember.* Though Kendell would probably experience the beer just as Endall had, confirming the level of Professor Yates's details seemed useful. "As we discussed earlier, I didn't toss you into hell."

"No, but you were one of the guards that kept me there. You don't seem the type to accept failure so lightly."

Endall hated having to explain her motives, but apparently, Colin needed convincing that she didn't have a hidden agenda. "Actually, I find it something of a relief not to be constantly keeping an eye on you. Agnes Delarosa believed the best place for you was isolated from everyone. Sanguine still thinks you should be erased from history. In my opinion, neither option is realistic. I'd hoped you might learn how to behave in society by passing through the seven gates, but apparently, I miscalculated your interest in me. Or was your escape a matter of not wanting to play by the rules?"

He ran his finger along the lip of his glass, which was filled with rum and Coke. "I've never been good at taking orders. You don't look the worse for wear."

She shrugged as if the spiritual damage of his busting through the seven gates didn't matter. "What's one more broken woman to you?"

"So our game is finished—no more controlling the curse, and no more banishments to hell?"

She looked around the courtyard as if seeing something he didn't. "You'll find this life is different than the one Agnes blew you out of with her hurricane. Success came easy to you back then. It won't now. We may not have been able to change your surroundings, but *you* are different."

He stopped playing with his glass. "Sanguine made a similar threat, but I can tell my history is intact. That must mean you still have the totem. I can feel it influencing my perception of people. Something about that voodoo fetish controls my destiny. What do you know?"

She was playing a bluff but one that worked well with both sides of his being. "Archibald Malveaux was a two-bit hustler before he stole Baron Samedi's cane. His business successes weren't earned. They were conjured. As a loa of the dead, he manipulated his family's genetics and fortunes, culminating in Lincoln Laroque. That titan of business had his accomplishments handed to him on a silver platter. You must see that nothing you've ever done has been due to your skills. Casting you into hell cut that umbilical cord to your source of power."

"You think just because you have that hunk of wood and glass you can influence my dominance over this world?"

She had the heady exhilaration of a prize fighter who had her opponent against the ropes. "I never said anything about that voodoo sculpture, but I find it interesting that you keep pursuing objects as the sources of your power. First, you thought you could rise through your family to gain control of their dynasty with the items cursed by

Marie Laveau, then you ruled the afterlife with Baron Samedi's cane, and now you hope to regain your command of life with the voodoo totem Delphine used to imprison Baron Malveaux. Your obsession with these magical items only proves your self-doubt. You're a fraud, and you know it. Now the rest of the world will know it too."

Quit while you're ahead. Endall heeded Kendell's advice and got up from the table, hoping he'd take the hint to leave.

Colin downed his drink as if he were seeking courage from the alcohol. "I didn't break out of hell just to become some wretched average Joe. You've proven nothing." He stormed out of the club like a jilted lover.

Endall fell back into her chair, quivering from the exchange. She tried finishing off her beer for strength. Her hand shook so badly that the dark liquid leaked out of her mouth, but the Kendell side of her glowed with pride. With Sanguine's help, they could ensure that every personal or business relationship Colin pursued with their cardboard people was doomed to failure.

The angelic-looking swamp witch floated down from the sky with her white wings spread so wide she nearly touched the brick walls. "You did good."

"You sound surprised." The slight irritation at being doubted helped calm Endall's nerves.

"Not surprised, but I think I understand a little better how you feel when I go off on one of my reckless ideas. All you had to do was reject his advances."

As Kendell, the simple rebuff might have been enough, but Endall wanted to squash the man's emotions like a bug, not just usher them outside. "He's still in our hell. Nothing's really changed regarding his incarceration, only the posters on the brick walls of the prison cell."

"I think I like this aggressive side of you. How do you want to orchestrate his failures?"

Endall caught Myles's eye behind the bar and raised her empty Abita bottle. He nodded and pulled out a couple of cold ones from the bar fridge. "How much control do you have over the voodoo-doll mirrors Delphine created?"

"You mean can I take over that fake Myles while he's making love to you?"

In her mind, she heard Kendell snicker, but the lustier Endall knew Sanguine's flirtations weren't so innocent. "Delphine used the unrestrained part of my being for this trip to hell. Back in life, Kendell can still access these wild characteristics, but here in hell, I'm relegated to only those parts of me that came along with the voodoo totem. So flirt with me at your own risk, sexy witch angel."

Sanguine had the shocked expression of a prepubescent girl who'd had her bluff called for *I'll show you mine if you show me yours*. "Point taken. I wouldn't want to take advantage of you, and it sounds like you're in about as much control of your desires as a drunk college freshman at a kegger. To answer your question, Polly let me use her voodoo interpretation to get that message to you. Anyone Delphine sent a voodoo doll to has control over what happens to their likeness here in hell. Professor Yates's projections of people, however, are completely under our control. They're kind of on autopilot until we take over."

Cardboard Myles set the three bottles on the table and took a seat. "What are you two talking about?"

Endall wondered what would happen if she jumped his bones then and there. "Just figuring out how much of you is real and how much imaginary."

He took a long drink of his beer while looking at her over the bottle. "How real is anyone we meet?"

At least conducting a philosophical conversation with what amounted to a sock puppet might help Kendell know how well the simulation was working. "First things first. Is Myles operating you, or are you on autopilot?"

He looked to be savoring his beer. "Ever feel like you're just going through the motions in life? You could be engaged, but you chose not to? I only know myself. I'm based on the person you know. My mind drifts along until someone comes along that makes me want to wake up from my complacency."

Sanguine put down her empty bottle. "Sounds like Myles, but he usually answers your questions in a more direct fashion. That vague answer sounds more like how he'd talk to me when he doesn't really want to."

Endall nodded. "So if someone responds to a question by asking another question, that person is not really engaged?"

Sanguine shrugged her wings. "In my experience, when someone deflects a question, they either don't have an answer or aren't interested in the topic."

Neither seemed plausible to Endall. Cardboard Myles had asked questions that were meant to engage, not deflect. "Everyone just goes through the motions at some point."

Myles started pulling the label from the bottle the way he sometimes did when bored. "What you really want to know is if I'm self-aware. I'm not sure I can answer that question. If I think hard enough, I call in the part of me in reality. That doesn't really qualify as self-aware as I'm focusing on my true being, not this projection. Do characters on the movie screen know themselves?"

"No," Sanguine said. "But you're not a recording."

He got up and collected the empty bottles. "True. I'm just a bartender in a play."

15

*C*olin spent the next three weeks trying to reacclimate to life. Nothing he did seemed to work. Past business associates wouldn't take his calls, not that he blamed them. A call from Lincoln Laroque's office used to mean a hostile takeover. Now that word had gotten out about the bank cutting off his access to unlimited funds, the city's CEOs didn't even have fear as a motivation to answer his calls. He tossed the stack of folders he'd been reading onto his desk. Like everything else he tried, they failed to do as he intended—they skidded across the glass and disgorged their contents all over the marble floor. *Fuck.*

He pressed the intercom button. "Claire, come pick up this mess."

There was no answer from the outer office. Irritation was becoming a constant reminder of how much he hated people, though their presence beat their absence. Instead of storming into the receptionist's office to yell at her for her negligence in not answering his summons, he turned to the wall of windows. He raised his hands, hoping to see his cloud of bats. As he expected, they didn't materialize.

One of his biggest lessons, having returned to life, was that business bored him to death. *If only that were literally true.*

He got out of his office chair, walked over the scattered papers, grabbed the iron walking stick he'd fashioned in hell, and exited his office.

Claire was busy typing something on her computer.

"Didn't you hear me on the intercom? My office is a mess. Clean it up."

She hit a key, and a page ejected from the printer. Without saying a word, she handed him her resignation.

"Perfect." He tossed the paper onto her desk and headed for the elevator.

He fumed the entire way down. She'd been a good secretary, but after four years of her working for him, he couldn't recall a single detail about her personal life. He wondered if it was even worth trying to replace her. Nothing about the business he'd worked so hard to build interested him any longer. The whole experience of being a titan in the community felt like it belonged to someone else. He'd been hell's devil, and now he couldn't even command a lowly office worker.

As he walked out of the elevator and through the lobby, he realized he had no idea where he was going. He just needed to walk. The iron cane cracked the marble tiles as he swung it along.

"Hey," the lobby receptionist yelled. "You're going to pay for that damage."

He doubted it was even worth explaining that he owned the building. "You're fired." He continued out of the front doors, not interested enough to turn back and see if she'd taken him seriously.

He spent the afternoon wandering the Warehouse District. The upscale restaurants and art galleries beat the Quarter's family-friendly food establishments and touristy gift shops, but he still looked in the dirty windows of each run-down building, hoping to see the completely empty rooms he remembered from hell. "How is it that I miss you, old witch?"

An elegant woman glanced at him as if he were a vagrant talking to himself. He tapped his ear, pretending he was wearing a hidden phone headset. Once she'd walked away, he looked over his long coat and purple paisley vest in the window's reflection. As the most powerful man in New Orleans, the eccentric attire had worked to distinguish him from the other rich businessmen. Now he just looked like another charlatan out to hustle a quick buck.

He checked his watch and was still somewhat amazed to see that the hands had moved. The simple magic of the earth's rotation, which he'd struggled so hard to accomplish in hell, was as accepted as breathing by everyone he passed on the street. *Fools.*

At the corner of Poydras and Magazine, he reluctantly turned toward the river. *Fuck you, Luther Noire.* Considering the power he'd wielded from the abandoned World Trade Center's vaults, the tower showed a disappointing lack of damage. *Even exploding a dimensional bomb in the heart of your cement tomb didn't faze you.* Back amongst the living, he'd lost his control of the structure. He didn't even know if the control room he'd built in the old circular restaurant still existed or was only a figment of his hell.

In the past, self-pity wasn't a condition he had tolerated, but that had been when he had a measure of control over his environment. The walk along Decatur to Frenchmen had become a nightly pilgrimage. Listening to Polly Urethane and the Strippers at the Scratchy Dog wasn't just about seeing Kendell again. Though she was the most real person he'd ever met, the fact that she wouldn't talk to him made being in her presence a physical pain. Masochism wasn't his objective. Something about the club drew him across town each night like a fishhook he couldn't dislodge.

He stopped in front of an empty lot with a concrete floor left over from a torn-down building. The smells of pizza and beer from the neighboring restaurant turned his stomach. Artists had set up tables in the vacant space to distinguish themselves from those willing to sell their wares on blankets along Decatur's sidewalks. He wandered in to kill a few minutes. Anything beat the air of desperation that accompanied being first in the door at the Scratchy Dog.

Hippie girls sold handmade soaps and jewelry made from feathers. Grungy dudes sat next to their paintings. Their attempts at nonchalant disdain failed to mask their need to make a sale. Torn, dirty jeans, paint-stained hands, and lack of personal hygiene told the true story.

He stood far enough from the displays to avoid being drawn into the banter between artists and their customers.

By the time he'd eavesdropped on the third encounter, he thought he could have scripted the exchange—always the same questions and answers. He wondered how the bohemian merchants kept from losing their minds at the monotony.

In the back corner, away from the noisy crowd of tourists, a series of black-and-white pictures made him stop. The camera exposures had been set for so long that everyone and every vehicle had disappeared from the image. All that was left on the film was the French Quarter devoid of life. The photographs gave him a sense of peace he hadn't noticed while in hell. He flipped through the stack of prints until he found one that had captured a vagrant hunched over on a park bench in Jackson Square. The homeless man had sat still for so long the extended exposure of him hadn't even blurred.

"That dude never did wake up. I was almost worried he'd died."

Colin turned to see a man holding a pizza slice. "You're the artist?"

"Is it art if I'm just capturing what I see?"

Colin suspected the question was his typical response, meant to draw potential customers in for the kill. "Probably not, but I'll take this print just the same." He pulled out his business card along with a wad of cash. "Frame it, and send it to my office."

The image continued to haunt Colin as he left the street gallery. People were like mannequins in a cheap department store—creepy things to be avoided. But when they were missing, the emptiness highlighted Colin's sense of life's futility. It didn't matter whether someone was a homeless beggar or the city's richest businessman. Status made no difference when a person was sitting on an empty bench in an empty world.

People were already milling around the Scratchy Dog's dance floor and ordering drinks when Colin made his way to the comfortable chair next to the sound-mixing console. Though he hadn't requested preferential treatment, somehow the clean, high-backed well-upholstered chair was always empty when he walked in. He preferred watching the gyrations of the college kids on the dance floor to joining in on the revelry. Being in the middle of the inevitable flirting and grinding only distracted him from the music. Not that Polly Urethane and the Strippers was a great band, but in spite of the activity and noise, he found peace in the club as if he belonged there, though he couldn't figure out why.

The band struck up the usual set list. He'd given up trying to make eye contact with Kendell. She would know he was there, just as he knew Myles was glaring at him from the bar. Some conflicts didn't require outward manifestations. Even being despised didn't disrupt his enjoyment of being present among people enjoying a night of dancing and drinking.

His appreciation wasn't solely about the music. When members did what they loved and patrons reflected the energy back to the stage, the feeling was palpable. He didn't need to work up a sweat to be a part of the experience.

As the night wore on, the dance floor filled with people. He stood to stretch his legs and get a better view of the women in their full musical glory. Polly was spinning around like Stevie Nicks, singing "Black Magic Woman." Her tambourine hit Kendell's elbow with such force that Kendell's guitar pick left her fingers and flew over the heads of the dancers. Colin caught the small triangle of plastic as if it were a Mardi Gras throw meant just for him.

~

OUT IN THE COURTYARD, Kendell focused on her beer to avoid making eye contact with the band.

"Fuck!" Polly wasn't so much pacing as stomping from one end of the courtyard to the other.

"It wasn't your fault, Polly," Kendell said.

"The hell it wasn't. If I hadn't been so carried away with the music, I wouldn't have hit your elbow. I know the way his mirror reality works. What I did here in life happened in hell. I let him through the fucking second gate."

Kendell got up to stop Polly's ranting. "You don't understand. It is not your fault. When we agreed to play again, we opened the door to Colin. The Endall side of me saw him not only enjoying the music but being a part of the whole scene. He passed the band's test. You couldn't deny him passage. Maybe it was inadvertent, but that's the way life works sometimes."

Polly sat on one of the metal chairs with her arms between her legs in a very unladylike fashion. "What do we do now?"

Up until then, Myles had been strangely quiet. "The problem is not just that he's passed through the second gate.

The question is, does he realize he passed through the second gate?"

Everyone went deathly quiet.

"If he did," Kendell said, "he would know he's still in hell."

Lynn stood next to the back door to make sure the private band meeting wasn't disturbed. "He might not know. He could just be holding onto the guitar pick as a memento of his night on the town. We all know he's got a little crush on Kendell. It's not like we set off fireworks just because he passes through one of the gates."

"Fuck!" Polly yelled again.

Myles stood and started retracing Polly's steps across the courtyard. "For once, I'm in complete agreement with Polly. We're fucked. We need to call in Sanguine. If Colin realizes the game we've been playing on him, Endall will be in serious trouble." He stopped in front of Kendell. "I know you want to keep an eye on Sanguine, but if I were Colin, kidnapping Endall would be my first move. Even if Lynn's right and he doesn't know he's passed through the gate, that's not a risk I'm willing to take with your soul. He's not dumb. He'll figure it out eventually."

"What would your second move be?" Kendell asked. "We didn't just give him a window into life—we gave him a virtual representation of what we're doing. A smart person might use that insight to figure out a way to escape. But he's also managed to pass through two of the seven gates— something we didn't really think would be possible. Would he try another prison break or continue working toward parole?"

Scraper downed the last of her Jameson's. "We're talking about Colin Malveaux. Has anyone considered that he may not want to leave?"

Kendell's head began to pound. "What do you mean?"

"He's the devil in a hell that we just made far too comfortable. In the arm-wrestling match for control of the World Trade Center, we tricked him into thinking he'd lost. Imagine him with"—she started ticking off items on her fingers—"one, unlimited power. Two, the supernatural skills he thought he'd lost. Three, full view of what's happening in life. And four, access to the woman of his dreams. Personally, I'm not sure that's a position I'd want to give up."

Kendell felt the Endall side of her cower like a frightened child. "I'd like to be brave and argue I need to stay in hell—that I can deal with Colin—but since it's just you guys, I'll confess Scraper's description scares the hell out of me."

Minerva leaned against the brick wall next to Scraper. "So we're just going to leave Sanguine to deal with Colin?"

Myles had lost some of the tenseness in his shoulders once Kendell had acquiesced to his idea of her leaving hell. "Maybe not. If we're worried that Colin has an advantage in seeing our mirrors in his hell, maybe we can use those same mirrors to our advantage. I'll need to talk to Professor Yates. Anyone have any thoughts on how to contact Sanguine?"

Kendell put her hand on his arm. "Leave that to Endall. Sanguine hasn't left her alone for more than half an hour since they teamed up in hell. I'm just worried about our avenging angel's response."

~

SANGUINE DID her best not to fly off in a rage while Endall explained the band's latest fuck up. "Those women are going to be the death of me."

"It's not their fault. No one thought Colin would actually learn anything. But now that he has…"

"I have to get you out of hell," Sanguine finished. "The lure only works so long as we keep the bait out of the mouth of the fish. And you, little one, he'd swallow whole."

Endall chewed on her thumbnail. "I hate leaving you alone to face Colin."

"We don't know if he has figured out about still being in hell. If I do have to face him, it will be without you moderating my actions. This realm is still our creation. He might have had control of his little Erector Set, but Luther once again has the batteries. And Luther has the keys to his playpen. Colin will have to do a lot of explaining to regain access to what he built."

"I so much wanted to live up to my name," Endall said, feeling more insecure than usual—the flip side of her enthusiasm onstage.

"Ending Colin once and for all was never your destiny. It's just nice to know there's a side of you that understands me better than Kendell lets on. Cheer up. We won—at least for the moment. Now, I'd better reunite you to her before

Myles inhabits that puppet of himself and does something stupid."

"When will you come home?" Endall asked.

She sounded so much like a little girl that Sanguine nearly lost control of her emotions. "I need to discover what Colin is up to. With my ability to read the future, I see three likely directions. Scraper could be right that Colin will accept his place in hell. All I have to do is stay out of his way, and he'll think he's in charge. That path branches off, though. Once he's figured out that those around him are just projections and not real people, boredom will set in. Then he becomes dangerous. He's not the type to slowly go through the gates once he becomes restless. On the other hand, for the most part, he doesn't give a damn about others, so he may not even care that they're not real. If he reaches that point of awareness but uncaring, and he and I cross paths, he might choose to attempt the remaining gates as his way of challenging me. He wouldn't be looking for redemption as much as proving he can defeat all of us."

Endall wrapped her arms around her stomach as if she were about to be sick. "Don't forget, Myles gave him the ability to empathize. Since he can see our improvement to hell, that characteristic must have kicked in. What's the third option?"

"If he sees you before I get you back to where you belong, he'll become obsessed with hunting you down. That look of vulnerability you're unable to hide will work like a drug on him. He'll become addicted to dominating you just as Baron Malveaux was addicted to turning women into prostitutes. If that happens, there will be no stopping him from his original idea of punching a hole between hell and life so he can partake of both worlds. That's why we have to get you out of here before he realizes he's still in hell."

Endall looked at the door and rocked in her chair. "Can you fly me to Delphine's shop?"

"He'd see us for sure from his penthouse. One look at me flying, and he'll know he's in hell."

Endall took a couple of deep breaths as if she were summoning all her courage. "Then we make a run for it." She was up and out the door before Sanguine could clear her wings from the metal chair.

Running through the streets of the Quarter with her five-foot-long wings trailing into every puddle-filled pothole made Sanguine quiver with the desire to take flight. Endall was easily a block ahead—much too far to protect her should Colin step out of the shadows and abduct her. But yelling for her to slow down might also call forth the devil.

Sanguine finally caught up with Endall at the front door of Scratch and Sniff. "And you call me reckless."

Endall turned away from the door. "Promise me you'll be okay. I'm not leaving until you do."

It warmed Sanguine's heart to know there was an aspect of Kendell that cared so much. "My plan is to stay out of his way for as long as possible. He needs to discover he's in hell on his own. Your team may be supplying the projected marionettes, but I'm in charge of the play. I'll keep him occupied for as long as I can with the puppets. If I sense that he's getting bored, I'll step in. The day he shows up at the convent to convince Miss Fleur he's ready for the third gate is the day I leave hell. I'll do my best to check in with you at Scratch and Sniff each day at five to let you know how things are progressing. Don't freak out if I miss a day or a week. If I'm not home sooner, tell Myles to expect me at Guinee's gate to hell in six months, no matter what happens with Colin."

"Where will you hide?"

Sanguine hated long goodbyes, especially when every moment was filled with peril. "I know this realm better than Colin ever will. Don't forget, I can see the future."

"You can only see what's ahead of you, literally and figuratively. If he sneaks up on you, your foresight won't do you a damn bit of good. I've slapped plenty of mosquitoes off my arm to know bugs have a blind spot. Don't get overconfident in your abilities."

Sanguine looked at the door, hoping Endall would take the hint. "I've also got every animal in New Orleans keeping an eye on him. Between my spies and my supernatural abilities, I'll be just fine. Now you have to go."

Endall finally nodded her agreement and turned back to the weathered door. "Don't take forever, okay?"

"We've both seen how fast Colin works through one of our plans."

The girl's snicker again reminded Sanguine of a little child. "I'll set a place for you at dinner—and will continue to do so until you come home."

~

With Kendell once again whole in spirit, Cheesecake

stopped her concerned whining, though curling up on Kendell's lap and growling with suspicion each time someone approached wasn't much better. Delphine had loyally performed her part in the plan, but to keep the peace, Kendell and Myles hadn't included her in the meeting at the apartment. *It's always one step toward trust then another step back with you, voodoo priestess.*

Professor Yates stood outside the open French doors on the balcony. "From our contacts with the embassies in hell, it would seem our projectors are working even better than planned—though, as Luther almost never leaves his office and the nuns don't like looking beyond the walls of their convent, I'm not putting too much trust in their assessments."

Kendell wondered if the embassies were of any use at all. "Whatever Colin is up to, he's steering clear of Scratch and Sniff and my seventh gate."

As usual, Polly spoke for the band. "We see him each night at the Scratchy Dog. Fortunately, he doesn't harass our version of Kendell, but he and Fake Myles have nearly come to blows a time or two. I guess that means he's at least somewhat invested in his reality."

Myles had Doughnut Hole snuggled next to him on the floor. "Not necessarily. I get the impression Colin would be even happier to mix it up with me if he thought I wasn't anything more than a walking and talking punching bag. As for my fifth gate behind the club, he's never ventured out there."

Kendell nudged Cheesecake but couldn't get her to move over. "I haven't been able to contact the Mary who watched the first gate since she let him pass. And the baron's kids who watch the third gate have also been out of touch, though I wouldn't expect to hear from them anyway with Baron Samedi keeping watch at the bank. Sanguine's in hell, so watching Colin through her sixth gate is meaningless. That only leaves Miss Fleur at the convent, and as Professor Yates said, the nuns don't like looking beyond their walls."

Lynn stopped playing with Cupcake and Muffin Top who, once free, promptly pounced on their brother, Doughnut Hole. "So we're flying blind and hoping Sanguine doesn't pull her avenging-angel routine? Tell me again how this was a win, because I'm not seeing it."

Myles took his hand off the black puppy so the three could tear around the furniture under Cheesecake's watchful supervision. "We have control of his power-generating plant. That's a big deal. Since he doesn't have my cane, he's limited to following the path we've laid out for him. We've deprived him of any way to break out of hell. Next, even though we're limited to keeping an eye on him with our gates, we do have other resources."

Professor Yates leaned against the doorframe, not entering the crowded living room. "It might be possible to modify my projections so we could see Colin. He is eating and drinking again now that time for him is moving forward. Since we're also projecting food and beverage, I should be able to spike the punch, as it were."

Myles started taking notes. "We don't want to give away that he's in hell. Whatever you do will have to be so subtle he couldn't detect it."

"Give me a few weeks to come up with something. I'll

need to check in with Luther as he's supplying the energy to our virtual reality."

Myles got back to his rundown for Lynn. "And most importantly, Sanguine is working within our plan. With her ability to see the future, she's not going to go off on some vigilante crusade. I'm not crazy about putting so much trust in her, but at least we do have a representative in hell. This time, she can fend for herself, so she won't be sapping your energy."

Lynn didn't look convinced. "It still seems like it's just a matter of time before he figures out our ploy and makes another attempt at passing through the gates. He's already manipulated his way past two of them. We really fucked up."

Myles sat back against the wall next to the couch. "As Kendell explained, that wasn't your fault. It was mine."

Kendell moved her hand from the arm of the couch to his shoulder. "You didn't do anything wrong."

"I gave him the ability to feel empathy. In hindsight, I think Marie Laveau was trying to warn me. Without being able to see life through another's eyes, he never would have appreciated what you women do onstage. I succeeded in selling him on his made-up reality, but in so doing, I gave him the key to your gate."

Myles wasn't going to like her take on Colin's evolution, but Kendell knew she was right. "It's called growth," she said. "You made Colin more human and not just the devil he wanted to be. The question is, how does he deal with seeing people as more than just playthings?"

16

Colin sat in his office chair and mindlessly played the guitar pick between his fingers like a coin. Something had changed. He had the giddy excitement he used to feel when buying out a competitor. The photograph that leaned against the wall tempered his adrenaline-fueled lust for action. He had pulled off the butcher paper but hadn't hung the print.

The homeless man had just sat on the bench while life swirled around him. If Colin focused hard enough, he could just make out the ghostly image of an elegantly dressed woman who passed the wretch without even turning her head.

Colin's connection to the image wasn't just based on its similarity to his former hell. He'd prided himself on being a shark—constantly on the move. Life and business were intertwined, and he needed to devour to survive. The stillness of the old black man in the rumpled and tattered clothing defied every instinct that had given Colin's old life meaning. And yet he saw himself as that vagrant.

People had been little more than breezes that barely ruffled Colin's well-tailored identity, just as the rush around the vagrant in the photograph failed to make any impression at all on him. For Colin, the hell the swamp witch had created carried with it a sense of peace.

"So what am I supposed to do now, old man?" Colin tossed the guitar pick onto his desk. It spun around and aimed at the photograph as if that was supposed to be an answer.

"Sorry, I'm not a statue, but I'm also no longer a shark. I suppose that means my answer no longer can be found inside this glass cage."

He got up and looked around his office for what he suspected would be the last time. The mementoes of his business conquests lined the shelves. His victories had been as meaningless as the hunks of glass and metal that marked his achievements like some kid's baseball trophies. He thumbed through the pile of pages he'd written documenting his observations in hell. They read like the ramblings of a madman. Only the photograph and guitar pick had any meaning for him, and both were still enigmas.

He pocketed the pick and left his office. The secretary's desk remained vacant. "Just as well."

He wandered down to Lafayette Square and sat at the base of the sculpture of Henry Clay to consider his options. The sprawling Gallier Hall that had been used as City Hall during Baron Malveaux's lifetime reminded Colin of his mother's desire for him to enter politics. That prospect carried no interest for him in life, death, or this strange continuation of his existence. Office buildings towered over the park, but they all looked tiny next to his.

At the edge of the park, a lone trumpeter played a haunting jazz number. As a teenager, Lincoln—now Colin— had longed to be an artist. Though he maintained an appreciation for creative endeavors, that life had eluded his grasp. He leaned back against the cold marble of the statue's base and savored the music. The playing was as near to perfect as he could imagine. *Too perfect.*

Like not wanting to wake from a dream, Colin dared not move a muscle while the thought took shape. The night before, while listening to Kendell, he'd marveled at her ability to slightly change the song with each playing. Perfection wasn't her aim. The variations weren't mistakes. They were life. What he was hearing from the trumpeter was more like a recording.

He fingered the guitar pick in his pocket. He'd been given an answer, but he'd let the noise of his life drown out the message.

When he opened his eyes and looked up, he saw a lone bat flying toward the Quarter. "I'm still in hell."

BOOK LIST

Technopia Series:
(writing as Greg Chase)
Creation
Evolution
Damnation
Salvation

The Malveaux Curse Mysteries :
(writing as G.A. Chase)
Dog Days of Voodoo
You, Me, and the Voodoo Queen
Oops! I Voodooed Again
Voodoo You Love
Voodoo You Think You Are
Love Me Like Voodoo

Other Stories
Through the Lens

ABOUT THE AUTHOR

G.A. Chase is the pen name for Greg Chase. He is a science fiction and paranormal author living in New Orleans with his wife, fellow author Deanna Chase, and their two shih tzu dogs. On any given day you can find him behind his computer, people watching in the quarter, or out in his studio creating stories in glass. His glass work can be found at www.chase-designs.com.

www.gregchaseauthor.com

www.ingramcontent.com/pod-product-compliance
Lightning Source LLC
Chambersburg PA
CBHW020324200626
46814CB00006BB/2402